ALBANY HOUSE
PART FIVE
LOOKING FOR ANNA

Nigel Heath

ISBN: 9798362162238

My grateful thanks in the preparation of Albany House are due to Marc Bessant Design, Mary Watts, Alexandra Bridger and my wife, Jenny Davis, for literary support, to artist Maureen Langford for the cover picture and to my walking companion and poet, Peter Gibbs, for his technical support. Peter's poetry anthology, Let The Good Rhymes Roll, is also published on Amazon.

Chapter 1

It was a miserably grey late November afternoon and the Jameson clan were driving over from Little Oreford to the home of their much-respected family solicitor, Claud Eustace Long, for the reading of the wills of their life-long friends and business partners Robin and Margo Lloyd.
It had all happened so quickly, Claude mused as he sat behind the polished wooden desk in his comfortably furnished, booklined library with a semi-circle of empty chairs placed in front of him, waiting for the family to arrive.
Margo, now in her seventy-seventh year, and still remarkably active and full of life, had suddenly taken to her bed with a bad bout of the flu, which had quickly turned to pneumonia and she'd died late the following evening, having been rushed into the County General Hospital. Being so suddenly and unexpectedly parted from his soulmate had naturally devastated her older brother Robin. There was nothing that could be termed unusual about their brother and sister relationship because there had been partners in both their lives, but somehow things had never really worked out for either of them. After highly successful careers in London, they had gone back to live in their childhood home,

picturesque Wisteria Cottage, beside the village green in the small North Devon village of Little Oreford.
Margo's unexpected death stunned and deeply saddened Laura and Ben Jameson. As a young family, they'd only been able to move into Albany House, the nearby Victorian rectory, thanks to Margo and Robin's generosity.
But worse was to follow when two weeks later, and the day before her planned funeral at the village's St Michael's Parish Church, Ben found Robin sitting slumped in his favourite armchair having taken a massive overdose.
'I'm so sorry everyone, but I couldn't face tomorrow or the rest of my life without her,' his brief suicide note read.
The loss of her dearest life-long friends, so soon after one another, deeply shocked Charlie Andrews, ne Potter, the Jameson family matriarch and she had taken to her bed at nearby Little Oreford Court, beside herself with grief.
Laura and her twin sister Corinne, faced with the dilemma of going ahead with Margo's funeral, or of postponing it until after Robin's body had been released following the inevitable inquest, now sought the advice of George Rollings. He was the tall, reed thin family

undertaker in the nearby market town of Draymarket. George, whose whole persona was one of care and concern, suggested that if the family wanted a postponement in order to have a joint funeral, then that could easily be arranged as it would spare them all a double ordeal.

So just after 3.30pm, following the private funeral and interment in the same grave at St Michael's, a mostly silent Jameson family were making their way in convoy though, now gloomy, and bare branched wooded lanes towards the nearby village of Yardley Upton. All were locked in their own personal memories of their two most kind and generous friends, who had both had such a profoundly positive effect on all of their lives.

Laura and Ben were travelling in the first car with their son Luke and his wife Roxanne, now both lecturers in climatology, who had travelled down from London to attend the funeral.

They had left their three-year-old son Luca with his grandpa, former Harley Street consultant Dr Albert Flavell. Following on behind were Corinne and her husband Michael, who were going on to have supper with her best friend Alicia Randall and her entertaining Canadian husband Shaun. They lived with their two children at The Woodlands, a substantial Victorian

mansion set in wooded grounds overlooking Draymarket.
Occupying the third car were Laura and Ben's daughter Lottie and her husband Andy. He was the award-winning Michelin Star Head Chef at The Oreford Inn, the Jameson family-owned country pub with rooms in Little Oreford. They had left their ten-year-old twins Jack and Hannah with their great grandmother Charlie to hopefully help take her mind off her tragic loss.
She was not alone there because The Oreford's Deputy Manager Annie Smart and her professional chauffeur husband Bob lived in an apartment above the former stables with their four-year-old daughter Olivier.
It had been capital provided by Robin and Margo, following the sale of their 1960s acquired homes beside the Thames in Richmond and in Central London for a total of nine million pounds that had funded the acquisition of Albany House, which they'd rented to their then young friends Laura and Ben for a nominal £100 a year. The Lloyds went on to buy, refurbish and reopen The Oreford Inn, which had been closed for years, and invited Laura's sister Corinne to manage it. This was followed by the purchase of the village's fire damaged Old Mill House and adjoining centuries old mill, which Laura's husband Ben restored, partly with their cash, as

well as heritage grants and went on to reopen and run as a Heritage Centre with craft workshops.
Robin and Margo had always promised that all their properties would pass, to Laura, Ben and Corinne on their deaths with sums for Luke and Lottie and the Jameson family had always taken that completely for granted. But would the wills, about to be read by their trusted family solicitor Claude Eustace Long, actually confirm this? That frightening thought suddenly floated into Ben's mind as they drove towards their solicitor's home. The later acquired Cheringford Arms would be safe because that had been purchased through the Jameson Family Trust Fund, Ben rationalised. The fund had been set up by the Lloyds and Charlie so that they could watch Laura, Ben and Corinne take advantage of part of their wealth during their life-times. Besides The Cheringford, the fund had also financed the acquisition of the five satellite guest houses, so they would also be OK, Ben reassured himself.
Claude Eustace Long always enjoyed the will reading ritual because it placed him centre stage, which pleased him because he was a bit of a showman at heart. He'd vowed never to fully retire because he loved the law, he loved his vast library of legal reference books and, most of all, he loved his life as a self- appointed country squire

living in a small Georgian pile on the wooded hillside overlooking Yardly Upton.
He found studying the looks of anticipation on the will recipients faces to be utterly fascinating, especially on the occasions when hopes were dashed or windfalls surprisingly reaped.
Having been gifted with a photographic memory, Claude could easily recall most of the terms of the wills he'd prepared for his more important clients and the Lloyds were no exception.
But he had no idea of the contents of a large sealed envelope handed to him by Robin with the strict instruction that it was not to be opened until after both he and Margo had passed away.
Now the reading of the contents of that envelope would be most interesting, he mused.
The grandfather clock, standing in the corner of his study, chimed four when, with the family seated in front of him, Claude ceremonially picked up a solid silver Victorian paper knife, opened the first of three envelopes on the desk in front of him and slowly drew out Margo's will. The light beyond the small mullioned windows had already started fading because it was such a miserable afternoon and this had accentuated the warmth and glow of the room with its subtle lighting and faint aroma of old

books. For some reason, Ben imagined Claude wearing a barrister's wig and about to dip his quill pen into an ink pot, but the image faded as he began to speak. First came a number of small bequeaths to the various charities which Margo had supported over the years and then a much larger donation of £100,000 to the child literacy charitable foundation she'd helped establish during her years as Chief Executive of a home counties library service. "I further bequeath the sum of £250,000 each to Luke and Lottie, who have brought so much joy into our lives as the honorary grandchildren neither Robin nor I ever had," Claud read. Luke squeezed Roxanne's hand at the prospect of the sizeable chunk they could now pay off their hefty mortgage, while Lottie glimpsed the chance of her and Andy buying a home of their own. "We come now to the final terms of Margaret Jane Lloyds will," announced Claude, pausing for effect, while returning his eyes to the document.
"I leave the remainder of my estate to the safe keeping of my brother, Robin Anthony Lloyd, unless he has predeceased me, and in which case, Laura and Ben Jameson and Corinne Potter, will each receive £750,000." Claude slowly put down the document and calmly observed the perplexed looks on the faces of his audience as they groped to come to terms with the

staggeringly large size of the legacy and the fact that, as Robin had now taken his own life, they would not be having to wait for their inheritance. “Might I offer a word of explanation at this juncture as to the substantial size of this legacy, as I have been the Lloyds’ solicitor, and might I say also friend, over many years,” said Claude coming to their rescue. “Yes, please do,” invited Ben, taking command of the situation.

“Robin and Margo first came to see me some thirty years ago, not long after I had gained my legal qualifications and had set up my practice in Draymarket. They had recently sold the London homes they had bought in the 1960s for a considerable sum and had, as you all know, taken early retirement and moved back to their childhood home in Little Oreford. Margo, as you may also know, always deferred to Robin when it came to financial matters and he skilfully managed their joint funds, guided first by a close friend from university days, whose trusted financial service mantel was later taken on by his son, whom Robin had known since he was a child. The long and the short of it is, that the considerable sum accrued from their house sales in the late 1980’s and later partly used for the acquisition of Albany House, The Oreford Inn and the Old Mill and for the setting up of your family trust fund, has still grown to circa £5 million.”

Claude paused to take in the looks of surprise and astonishment on the faces of his audience. "I have been a party to all this because having first acted for them over the initial purchase of the three properties, I was then asked by Robin for my opinion on certain investment opportunities he was considering, and this was because I had studied financial law as part of my legal training. He would pop into my chambers in Draymarket High Street when he had something on his mind and we'd stroll over to The Carpenters for lunch and to talk over his latest prospect," Claude explained. This was a revelation for Laura and Ben because it opened up an unexpected window on a part of 'Uncle Robin's' life they knew absolutely nothing about, even though they had been such close friends. "It was probably five years ago that Robin and Margo came over to see me here saying it was about time they made their wills," Claude continued.

"We had a long discussion, and while it was made clear that virtually all their joint assets were to come to you, that was not to be until after they had both passed away, hence the clause in Margo's will about most of her estate passing to Robin unless he had predeceased her." Claude paused again to allow the Jameson family members to mentally catch up with him.

"So as Margo died first, you might then have waited some years before receiving her bequeath to you, although that would not have affected the sums left to you Luke and Lottie. However, as you will by now have realised, following Robin's sad and untimely death, you now receive the £750,000 legacies left to you by Margo, plus any further bequeaths in Robin's will that I am now about to read to you," said Claude, again picking up the paper knife and beginning to open a second envelope. Now the Jameson family sat in total suspense, hardly taking notice of the number of modest bequests Robin was making to the charities he had supported over many years, as they waited for Claude to reach the heart of the will. "Before moving on to my more substantial bequests," Claude read, "I leave the sum of £250,000, specifically to meet the repair and running costs of our dear St Michael's Church in which, although not being a member of the congregation, I have spent many hours, in quiet contemplation." Laura and Ben glanced at one another, taken completely by surprise by Robin's' bequest. His parents had been agnostics, or so he had told them, and neither he nor Margo had ever shown more than a passing interest in the village church, yet he had been sitting quietly in there all these years and they'd never known. Claude noted the look of surprise on Laura's face over the gift to the church, but that was nothing compared with what he knew was to come. "As you know, I have always been interested in town planning having been one of the civil servants responsible for advising the Minister for Housing," Claude continued. Most of his clients simply listed their bequests with no more than a token explanation, but that was certainly not so in Robin's case, he thought, as he slowly carried on reading.

"I guess it was some inner desire to improve people's lives by providing homes in decent environments, but where it came from, I have completely no idea," Claude read. "I think it was this desire that motivated me to create my perfect scale model of Little Oreford in our cottage garden," Robin explained.

Listening to their much-loved 'Uncle Robin,' talking now from beyond the grave, both Luke and Lottie were instantly transported back to a sunny morning in their young lives which neither of them would ever forget. It was a school in service training day, so their mum had taken them up to Little Oreford to visit Margo and Robin, whom she'd recently met, and there in the back garden to their surprise and delight Robin had shown them his model village. Within minutes they were in his workshop helping to make a swing for the tree in the front garden of Albany House, which Robin' and Margo were soon to buy and rent to their parents, so that mum could fulfil her cherished dream of making the old rectory their family home.

"It has been a continuing source of joy for both Margo and I that our honorary great grandchildren,' Jack and Hannah, have come over regularly with Lottie and have become my new little helpers, encouraging me to restore the village." Claude paused to turn the page. "So, it occurred to Margo and I, that as Lottie and Andy do not yet have a family home of their own, then we should also leave them Wisteria Cottage to move into when the time is right."

Again, Claude paused to allow time for his audience to assimilate the news that would certainly have come as a complete surprise to the whole Jameson family. But before anyone had time to consider the implications of this bequest, Claude was moving swiftly on, as if he was a conductor playing with their emotions. "However, if Lottie and Andy do accept this bequest, then it will be only fair for the property to be valued and the sum of that valuation to be bequeathed to Luke and Roxanne. Should they decide otherwise, then Wisteria Cottage will become the property of the Jameson Family Trust Fund."

Prior to this point, it seemed as if the entire family had climbed aboard an emotional rollercoaster. While Lottie and Andy's spirits had soared at the prospect of having the cottage, both Luke and Roxanne felt shocked and upset at losing out. Laura and Ben both immediately feared ructions between the haves and the have nots and then with his next sentence dear old Robin had made everything right again.

Laura had begun wondering how, after losing both her best friends, her mum would feel about Lottie, Andy and her much loved great grandchildren leaving Little Oreford Court. 'But let's not meet trouble half way,' she told herself. Corrine, who was sitting beside her, was delighted at the prosect of inheriting £750,000. One thing was for sure and that was that she and Michael would be finding a spacious new home of their own sooner rather than later. They should really have moved ages ago, but what with her running The Oreford and Michael's earlier involvement with the Cheringford Arms restoration project and supervising its kitchen, they'd never gotten around to it.

Now Claude was again turning the page and poised to deliver what he considered the will's most surprising and sure to be completely unexpected provisions. "As I am confident that the £750,000 each that my much-loved

sister, Margo, has left to you Laura, Ben and Corinne, will be more than suffice to meet your personal needs, I bequeath £1 million to the Jameson Family Trust Fund for the furtherance of your business enterprises.
A further £750,000 from my estate will go into a new Jameson Family Charitable Trust Fund to be established and administered by my lawyer and friend, Claude Eustace Long, and to be used for good and charitable works as you all see fit."
Claude put down the document, took off his glasses and looked at them all, blinking owl-like. "So, I guess we will all have to sing for our supper, so to speak. But I am sure we can take our time before deciding how best to fulfil Robin's wishes and you should know that I will be playing my part purely in an honorary capacity," he said. "But as there is still one more document relating to Robin's will to be read, I thought we might take a short break for some light refreshments." Getting slowly to his feet, he gestured towards the large table that unseen hands had now quietly laid out with a selection of sandwiches and savouries, two large pots of tea, wines and soft drinks, at the far end of the room and accessed by another door. "This is most welcome Claude because I was beginning to flag," admitted Ben. "Might I ask if you know what's in the remaining envelope?" he enquired. "I

have no idea," came the surprising reply. Plates piled high in hand because everyone was hungry following the ordeal of the funeral and the intensity of the will reading, Lottie and Andy and Luke and Roxanne were standing together discussing their joint good fortune. "I assume you will be moving into Wisteria Cottage," Luke was saying to his sister. "I guess we will, won't we Andy? although I wouldn't want to upset grannie quite yet, at least until she's started getting over losing Robin and "Well," she told him. "Well, it's certainly going to be OK with us because the cash value of the cottage, together with 'Auntie Margo's' separate £250,000 bequest means we'll be able to pay off our mortgage," said Luke. Roxanne was not so sure they should pay all the money off their mortgage, but she'd have to discuss that with Luke later.
It was Robin's new charitable trust, coming so completely out of the blue, that was being briefly discussed by Laura, Ben and Corinne and the conclusion was that they should meet up with Claude to discuss the matter in a couple of weeks or so, when things had all settled down a bit. Michael was not party to the conversation having gone off to use the nearby toilet and was now perusing the selection of watercolours displayed on the wall at the far end of the

study. “They are rather fine, aren’t they?” said Claude, coming over to join him. “My favourite is this one,” said Michael, drawing his attention to a large picture of a sandy beach scene with spring flowers scattered amid wild grasses all around a deserted bay, “Yes, it is rather lovely and so real that I can feel myself beginning to relax just looking at it,” Claude agreed. “It’s on the main island of St Mary’s in the Isles of Scilly, twenty-eight miles off Land’s End, which I discovered some years ago and has been my summer escape ever since.
This is the original, but I know there are some very high-quality prints available should you want one,” he said. “I don’t, but I do know that Laura and Ben love watercolours and I think I might suggest to Corinne that we get them one for Christmas.” Claude hesitated. “No on second thoughts, don’t do that because they can have this one as a token of the high esteem in which I hold the Jameson family,” he said. “That is most generous of you Claude, but are you sure?” asked Michael. “Yes, I am sure, but now I think it’s time wc reconvened to hear what instructions, or other further matters Robin has to impart to you all. now that everyone has cleared their plates.”

Chapter 2

The year was 1966 and the location was a leafy suburb on a convenient tube line into central London, where Robin Anthony Lloyd had just acquired a run-down Edwardian villa for the princely sum of £4.950. It was a huge sum of money, but luckily, he had a favourite bachelor uncle, who lent him the deposit on lengthy interest free repayment terms.

His parents, both teachers, had inherited the family cottage beside the green in the picturesque North Devon village of Little Oreford, from his maternal grandmother and were always short of cash, so they would never have been able to help.

Fortunately for Robin's sister Margaret, who always insisted on being called Margo, Uncle Horace, who was something in the city, felt similarly obliged to help her when she found her own property close to the Thames in Richmond.

While Robin, had studied economics at Oxford, and joined the Civil Service, working in the Department of Housing, his equally intelligent sister, decided that university was not for her and had gone into the library service. Brother and sister had always been close since

childhood days, when they formed a then inseparable bond with the Rector of Little Oreford's wayward daughter, Charlie Potter, and spent almost all their free time with her roaming the fields and woods around the village.
They did not see so much of one another, or indeed anything of Charlie, after starting out on their respective careers because they were both busy at work and making new friends.
Not long after moving to Richmond, Margo formed a close friendship with a colleague called Rachael. They spent most of their free time together, going clubbing in central London at the weekends on the look-out for boys with whom to pair up.
They never dated young men, who did not have an eligible friend, however attracted they were, because that would not be fair, and besides, it was far more of a laugh being in a foursome.
While Margo had always been quite grounded and level headed, Rachael Jefferson, who had a wealthy family background, was stunningly attractive and made all heads turn whenever she walked into a club or bar. She was also highly strung, neurotic and had possessive traits she recognised, but had the knack of keeping the lid on until she grew tired of the particular boy she had

partnered up with, after which their foursomes normally fell apart. Rachael was the leader, like Charlie had always been back home in Little Oreford in Margo's childhood days, so perhaps in some way, that was the reason why she was content to follow, although she knew her own mind and would happily say 'no' when something did not suit her.

The two young women had been inseparable for almost a year when, Margo bought her property and decided to throw a housewarming party, and that was when her friendship with Rachael and her weekend clubbing suddenly came to an abrupt end. For Robin came along, locked eyes with Rachael, while being introduced by Margo and the chemistry fizzing between them hit the ceiling. Within days, she'd moved out of her flat and in with Robin, who could not help himself when it came to heeding his sister's dire warnings as to what Rachael was really like.

Margo now lost her best friend and, by default, became estranged from her dear brother and was left feeling deserted, lonely and bitter towards them both and it was many months before she began to get over it.

"Of course, as my sister had predicted, it did not work out, and over the next couple of years we were hopelessly and helplessly lost in a tumultuous love, hate relationship," explained Robin in the letter that Claude had produced from the third envelope and was reading to them in an atmosphere so tense that it might have been be sliced through with his Victorian paper knife.

"It was the classic we could not live together and yet we could not live without one another. She would suddenly up and leave for weeks on end and then return, right out of the blue, with no explanations as to where she had gone and what she had been doing and our ritual dance would begin all over again.

Heaven knows how she supported herself because, although she resigned from the library not long after moving in with me, she never seemed to be short of money. But gradually her absences grew longer until she finally disappeared from my life altogether and I quietly got on with my career, half hoping she'd come back, but also wondering what on earth I would do if she did. I'd really hurt Margo, which I bitterly regretted, and we almost completely lost touch only hearing about what was going on in one another's lives on our visits home to see our parents.

"Then, one autumn afternoon, it must have been at least six years later, there was a knock at the door and there she stood with a child, probably aged about four, whom she introduced as my daughter Anna.

I could see she was in a highly emotional state, but she refused to come in and simply said she was planning a journey, but before she went, she just felt I should know the fair-haired little girl was mine. She was still a most attractive and well-dressed woman, but the intervening years had taken their toll.

I pleaded with her again to come in, but she said she could not and turned and walked away, leading the child by the hand.

It was an image that has stayed with me all my life.

I worried for months about what might have happened to them and couldn't bring myself to read the Evening Standard for weeks in case I'd see she'd jumped off a bridge into the Thames, or something awful like that, because I wouldn't have put it past her. I never saw Rachael again, but eventually I was relieved to receive a brief note from her saying she'd moved to Glastonbury in Somerset and that Anna was now attending a local junior school and had settled in and was doing well.

My career was really taking off and in the fullness of time, I managed to put it all behind me. Margo and I eventually became friends again, but Rachael was the one subject that was totally taboo. I suppose I began wondering in my later years if Anna, who'd be your age by now Laura and Corrine, really was my daughter and if so, what might have become of her. I guess that was because I was coming to the end of my three score years and ten and that was the one real issue that had never been resolved in my life. So, I am hoping that one of you will take on the task of finding out what happened to my child and so write the final chapter in my otherwise long and happy life.

If you are successful, then I have set aside the £250,000 residue of my estate as her inheritance, but if not, then that sum will revert to your new charitable trust."

Claude put the letter down on his desk and again took off his glasses and began polishing them with a small linen handkerchief. It was a ritual he mostly always performed when giving his clients a little time to absorb some important information he had just imparted to them. But the Jamesons all sat there quietly in front of him and no one moved. It was as if some spell had been cast over them, because everything they had been told over the past couple of hours was so thought- provoking that they were all suffering from complete emotional overload. It was Ben, who finally broke the spell, by getting slowly to his feet, thanking Claude for his hospitality and saying that everyone now had an awful lot to think about. There was a shuffling of chairs as they all followed suite, queuing to shake hands with their solicitor, before stepping slowly outside and instantly setting off the security lights, bathing them all in an uncompromising white light. Talking in subdued voices, the only topic of conversation was Robin and his beyond the grave revelation about his love child Anna. It was finally agreed that they would all reconvene for supper at Albany House the following evening to go over everything they had been told and to begin making some sort of plan for the future.

"So, changing the subject, how does it feel to have been left £750,000?" Michael" asked Corinne as they drove slowly away.

"I know one thing and that is I'll be off to Hendon Motors in Draymarket first thing in the morning to replace this old rust bucket with some top of the range four-by-four," she replied.

In truth, her midrange hatchback was not in that bad a condition, but small things had started annoying her, like a glove compartment lid that had developed an irritating rattle, and a boot that would no longer close without her slamming it down.

The reality was that she could easily afford a new car, but they'd both been so busy that she'd never gotten around to it.

“No being serious, inheriting all that money is almost too much to think about at the moment, but I guess we should keep quiet about it at Alicia’s this evening, at least for the time being,” she suggested.
Corinne and Michael spent at least one evening a month at Alicia and Shaun’s, as well as the occasional weekend, and were now regarded by their nine-year-old daughter Corina, who was Corinne’s Goddaughter, and her and sixteen-year-old son Anthony, as their honorary aunt and uncle. Alicia Randall, widow of county-wide estate agency boss, Royston Randall, had later married her former Canadian lover Shaun Morrison, but had decided to keep her own name. The estate agency had been acquired, just a few weeks before Royston’s tragic sudden death, by his close friend and wealthy hedge fund boss Mark Hammond. He'd initially been intensely ‘interested’ in Alicia, but when she eventually spurned his subtle advances, he’d sold on the chain in a fit of pique. “Luckily, Alicia had retained a ten per cent stake in the business, which netted her a cool £2.3 million when she sold her shares, and that was when she’d decided to ‘splash out’ on her indoor pool complete with jacuzzi, steam and changing rooms and large external hot tub.

Designing an extension that would dove-tail seamlessly onto the end of the mansion and would satisfy county planners had not been easy. But luckily, a new architectural practice had recently established itself in Draymarket and its boss, Siegfried Summers, had risen magnificently to the challenge. Alicia had found this slim, highly enthusiastic and nattily dressed man to be rather a dish and had spent quite a bit of her free time in his company, especially as Shaun had often been away on business during the design and construction period.
Her dream pool had a striking glass atrium roof and picture windows, which could be seamlessly opened by remote control during the summer to access a newly constructed patio, with magnificent woodland views.
It had become the norm for Corinne and Michael to stay over and that, after a swim and supper, when the kids were safely in bed, they would retire to the study, amply supplied with drinks, and enjoy a big screen catch up session with their close friends Jonathan and Chrissy in Toronto. Alicia met them at the door with an excited Corina by her side, but there was no sign of either Shaun or Anthony. "Where's the rest of our reception party?" asked Michael, who was carrying their overnight bag and a holdall containing wine and a bunch of supermarket flowers.

"It's just going to be the three of us tonight, plus Corina, I'm afraid because Anthony's not feeling very well and has taken himself off to bed, and Shaun's been delayed in central London and won't now be back until tomorrow so sends his apologies.

"Mum, can I show Auntie Corrine and Uncle Michael my new blow-up pool toy?" asked Corina, who was standing beside her.

"Can't it wait until we've had a cup of tea and some cake?"

"Please let me show them now," her daughter persisted.

"Oh! go on then, just while I'm making the tea and finding a vase for these lovely flowers Auntie Corinne and Uncle Michael have brought us."

Later, after they'd all been swimming with Michael spending most of his time towing Corina around on her new giant inflatable dolphin, Corinne sat at the kitchen table with a large glass of red wine talking to Alicia, who was making the final preparations for their supper. Michael was upstairs reading Corina her bedtime story.

"Is everything all right because you've seemed a bit preoccupied this evening?" Corinne asked.

"Well, no not really," replied Alicia, who had her back turned as she continued with her stir fry. "It's Shaun. He's missing Toronto terribly and says that as he's now had five years with me in England, that perhaps it's his turn for us to go back to his home."

"Oh! dear, but you spend the whole of your summer holidays with him at Rosedale and most Christmas and New Year's, so isn't that enough for him?" Corinne was beginning to see all sorts of trouble ahead, especially if her friend did not want to go.

"No, not really. It's all this business of absence making the heart grow fonder and, besides that, he really misses all the camaraderie he shared with Jonathan, because he's not really made any close men friends over here, apart from your Michael that is," she explained. "Oh dear!" said Corinne again. "So, what are you going to do?" she asked. "To tell you the truth, I just don't know. Corina adores her daddy and I don't think it would make much difference to her, but I'm certainly not so sure about Anthony.

Although he's grown up for his age and really quite adventurous, he'd still have so much to lose at such a critical time in his life. He's been a boarder with his best friend Michael at Camleigh College since he was a junior and they've already started exam preparations, and besides that, being taken away from Royston's classic car collection and from dear Bob, whose been his mentor ever since Royston died, is almost unthinkable."

Alicia turned to face Corinne with tears in her eyes. “I do love Shaun, but I can’t destroy Anthony’s life, so I don’t know what I am going to do.” she admitted.

Chapter 3

What to do about finding Robin's Anna was top of the agenda when the Jameson family reconvened at Albany House the following evening. Corinne and Michael had strolled across from the inn, Lottie and Andy had come over from Little Oreford Court, having left the twins with Charlie, but Luke and Roxanne had already driven back to London.

Laura had laid on a buffet supper and, as she and Ben were playing host, it was he who nominally took charge of their discussions. "We have the sad task of clearing the cottage and going through all Robin and Margo's things. I'm hoping that, as Robin and Rachael were so crazy on one another, then there may at least be some old photos, or letters amongst his papers, which might help us find out whatever happened to their love child," he said. "But I guess, of more immediate importance, we need to think about his incredible £1.5 million top-up for our family trust fund and the setting up of his new charitable trust. As you know, our funds, and those of yours Michael, were pretty much drained by the acquisition of The Cheringford, and the much larger than expected cost of extending and modernising it. So, do we now just sit back and let this new cash accrue a

modicum of interest, such as it is, or does anyone have any other ideas?" he asked. "Well seeing you've asked, then I do," said Michael. "I know, from what I've heard from you all in the past, that Robin always wanted the long abandoned red brick kennels on that patch of overgrown open ground beyond the church, to be restored and put to some use.
So, if we were to rebuild his model village on a larger scale and extend and convert the kennels to form a ticket office and café, we'd be creating a completely new stand-alone attraction to compliment the Old Mill House and generate even more business for The Oreford. So, what do you think?" he asked. "Michael that's a great idea, and, as you say, it actually ticks a lot of boxes. But I wonder if that's still church land, or actually belongs to someone else," Ben wondered.
Corinne was not quite so sure about it being such a good idea.
"It's also close to the allotments and are the allotment holders going to want a model village on their doorstep, spoiling their peace and quiet?" she asked. "And while I don't really want to pour more cold water over the idea, what about the parking, seeing we had to get permission from the parish council to use part of the village green for Luke and Roxanne's wedding? she pointed out. "All

that is true," Ben agreed. "So, what do you think Lottie and Andy?" he asked. "It sounds really exciting to me and I know the twins would absolutely love it, if those problems over the noise and the parking could be resolved," said Lottie.

The meeting broke up around ten, and as neither Corinne nor Michael felt like driving back to his rented house in Wixton, they strolled back across the village green to The Oreford and to her apartment above the old stables. In some ways it had seemed ridiculous to keep two homes going, as they had done since they'd wed three years earlier. But it was also quite practical with Michael running The Cheringford, just down the road, and she managing The Oreford. They'd lived for a short while in Rose Cottage, one of the five properties acquired by the Jameson Family Trust and converted for the B&B trade.

But then it felt unfair to go on depriving the trust of its income. "Now we have Margo's inheritance money, maybe it really is time we found a proper home of our own somewhere half way between here and Wixton," suggested Corinne as they climbed into bed.

It had been agreed that before driving back to The Cheringford the following morning, Michael would meet up with Ben and take a walk through the small woodland separating St Michael's from the old kennels site and then back via the lane, which also linked the allotments to the village. Corinne was right, the allotments were closer to the kennels than he'd realised, Ben conceded. It seemed ridiculous that he hadn't walked down there for years, despite the fact that The Old Mill House was so close by.

But they could still be screened by some effective tree planting and the visitor access problem could be solved by an extension of the church carpark to take at least another thirty vehicles, Michael pointed out. All in all, the difficulties Corinne had envisaged, could be overcome and the new model village project was definitely worth further consideration, they agreed.

The old kennels land ownership question was answered a couple of weeks later in an out of the blue phone call to Laura from the vicar of Draymarket and Priest in charge of St Michael's Little Oreford. It was the evangelically inclined Rev Martin Clark, who had taken Robin and Margo's funeral, and had created a lasting impression when he'd conducted Luke and Roxanne's wedding in the village church with much gusto some five years earlier.

"Dear Mrs Jameson, I immediately thought of you this morning when I opened my post to read a solicitor's

letter informing me that St Michael's is to receive the amazing donation of £250,000 towards its future upkeep from the estate of Mr Robin Lloyd.
I can't tell you just how grateful I am, especially when I recall that it was through your good offices that we also received that £30,000 donation around the time of your son's wedding from that most generous business contact of yours." Laura said that while she might have influenced the earlier donation, she had no prior knowledge of Mr Lloyd's bequest. "However, perhaps you can tell me whether or not the church happens to own that small patch of woodland beyond St Michael's, which also includes the old village kennels and surrounding patch of overgrown land. "Yes, indeed we do, but I'm afraid it has been rather a case of out of sight out of mind. We have been fighting a losing battle just to keep St Michael's churchyard in some sort of order, let alone caring for an old building hidden by the woodland beyond. Why are you interested might I ask?" Laura said she couldn't really talk about it now, but perhaps he might care to drop by for coffee after his 10am service on Sunday. The Rev Clark said he'd be delighted to do so and turned up to be introduced to Ben, Corinne and Michael, all of whom he recognised from the recent funeral. He listened with growing interest as Ben and

Michael carefully outlined their proposal. The more he heard, the more he was taken with the idea because instead of being a little used drain on church resources, he suddenly saw St Michael's taking centre stage once again.

"It's a splendid idea and perhaps you could create a new model village access path from the extended car park and through the churchyard, so encouraging visitors to pop into St Michael's, which has several very fine stained-glass windows and many other historic features," he suggested. "So where might we go from here?" asked Ben. "Ah well, even with my whole-hearted support, and of that you can now be assured, this might well be a fairly long and slow process. There will, of course, be the views of my, admittedly extremely small congregation to take into account, and although I never like meeting trouble half way, if they were to be strongly opposed, then we might end holding a Consistory Court," he warned them. "What's one of those when it's at home?" Ben asked. "It's a church court, presided over by a judge, appointed by a bishop, to rule over really contentious matters. They are quite rare, but I do luckily happen to have experience of one some years ago when I wanted to replace my church bells with recorded ones. This caused a real storm, even though the ones in my tower were becoming unsafe and it was going to cost a small fortune before they could be safely played again," he told them. "We're certainly in no hurry if a Consistory Court has to be held, because we'd also have to have plans drawn up seeking change of use for the site and that would then have to take its due course through the local planning system. But we wouldn't even begin that process until we'd had a green light from your church authorities." Ben assured him.

The Rev Clark said he be delighted to sound out his church warden's and then, if necessary, the bishop in complete confidence.

And on the question of confidence, perhaps it would be best if everyone kept the project under their hats for the time being.

Ben and Michael agreed, but because of his most welcome support they would probably set the ball rolling by getting an architect's view and thoughts on the project.

Chapter 4

That same Sunday morning in a fold in the rolling countryside, some thirty miles away, wealthy hedge fund boss, Mark Hammond, was currently in residence at The Manders, his classic Georgian pile.

His operation was based in London and Zurich, where he had a large penthouse and boardroom for meeting potential investors, and it was while attending an international conference on the state of the world's markets that he'd met his future wife at one of the endless round of cocktail parties.

Annette was a highly qualified financial personal assistant.

She quickly fell for this not unattractive and sophisticated older man, who commuted between London and Zurich in his own private jet.

He invited her to come and work for him, but what with their mutual attraction, one thing led to another and they wed and their son, Mark Junior, arrived just a little over nine months later.

While she had an excellent head for finance and was a good organise, she was also very artistic and a homemaker and quickly adapted to life at The Manders.

She took control of running the small country estate with

its excellent pheasant shoot, while setting about a major interior redecoration of the mansion which had definitely seen better days. The exotic paintings in the master bedroom, ended up on a bonfire within days of her arrival.

Annette accepted that her husband's being away from home a lot on business, came with the territory and now having her child to look after and much else to do, she was content.

But privately, Mark Hammond. was never content, which was probably why he'd become so successful and above all he did not like mysteries.

Completely unknown to his wife, there had been another highly attractive woman from Costa Rica, who had also been invited to The Manders. But she had walked out on him in highly embarrassing circumstances while they were attending a wedding. He later learned that she'd last been seen climbing into a taxi with another of the guests on his way back to London.

Under normal circumstances, most men in his position would have just let her go, but these were not normal circumstances because he'd recently been contacted, out of the blue, by a Costa Rican serious crime officer. He was seeking the whereabouts of a colleague, one, Chrissy Morales, who had been sent to Europe on an

assignment, some five years earlier under the cover name of Angelina Perez and had not been heard of since. “So how did you obtain my private number and why do you think I should know anything about this woman?” asked Mark. He was certainly completely unprepared for the answer.
“That is easily explained Sen Hammond, because you and your earlier dealings with the Jimarenal Corporation here in Costa Rica were the subject of her under cover enquiries and we are hoping, for your sake, that you have a reasonable explanation as to what has become of her.” There was an implied menace in this caller’s voice. Mark’s heart began thumping and he felt a panic rising from the pit of his stomach as he tried desperately to remain calm. “But she and I parted company, what must be five years ago, so why on earth have you waited until now to call me?
It was a perfectly reasonable question. “That is because, Sen Hammond, it is only recently that certain information has come to light, confirming that you were completely unaware that the millions of dollars the corporation poured into your fund were the proceeds of illegal drug production throughout Central and South America. So, to put it quite bluntly, you were a prime suspect in this, admittedly long running investigation.”

This officer spoke, excellent English and from all that he had said so far, there really was no further need to question his identity. Mark was now highly relieved at being so unexpectedly let off this particularly nasty hook that had been clinging on in the back of his mind for years. He told how Angelina Perez had completely taken him in. She had come to England at his expense to attend a wedding and had left him there and disappeared without trace.

"That being the case, Sen Hammond, and because you are a man of considerable resource, might we now leave it in your capable hands to establish what has become of our missing operative? You can then call me back on my office number here in San Jose," he instructed.

Mark had secretly worried for years there had been something not quite on the level about all those millions of dollars the Jimarenal Corporation had poured into his fund to help establish it in those early days. He willingly agreed to do whatever he could to find out what had become of the woman, who had made such a fool of him in return for her sexual favours.

To think he'd set her up in an expensive apartment in Zurich and she'd also had a completely free run of his penthouse and boardroom.

So, goodness knows what she might have got up to. Annoyingly, he could not question Jacob Johnson, who had long been in charge of the Head Office suite at the time, because he had suddenly up and left over a year ago. He certainly had some scores to settle with that woman, who'd so cleverly deceived him and the fact that she had deserted her post meant she was probably in trouble with her people back home in Costa Rica. Finding out exactly what had happened to her and reporting back to her boss would pay her back, so what he needed now was a private investigator.

It was late afternoon in Toronto and Chrissy Morales and her four-year-old daughter Sophia had just returned from a shopping expedition downtown. The little girl had dark hair and striking features, so much so, that her father, successful city lawyer, Jonathan Meyer, sometimes wondered where he fitted into the picture. She had shown signs of having a remarkable intelligence even at that young age, but he couldn't really claim that as being his contribution because Chrissy was also extremely smart.

But no matter because Jonathan adored his daughter and was very much in love with his much younger and most attractive wife. The two had met at a family wedding in the UK where he had relations in the small

North Devon village of Little Oreford. Jonathan had flown over there for a holiday with his close friend, Shaun Morrison, who owned the substantial house next door to his in the leafy suburb of Rosedale.
Jonathan invited Chrissy back to Toronto for a holiday, but she'd never left and almost before he knew it, he had become a dad, having earlier escaped from a relationship with one of his much younger and highly ambitious business partners. That was the wonderful thing about Chrissy because she was so easy going and a brilliant cook, a skill she'd discovered after first being let loose in his kitchen.
Jonathan was in a particularly good mood that late November afternoon because Shaun, who had lived in the UK for the past five years with his wife Alicia, nine-year-old daughter Corina and sixteen-year-old step son Anthony, was coming home for Christmas. Soon Shaun's long-standing live in housekeepers Lewis and Lois would be busy making the place ready for the homecoming. When Shaun had decided to move to the UK to be with Alicia, Jonathan had known he was really going to miss his best friend and next-door neighbour, but then again, perhaps it was not going to be a permanent arrangement because he was keeping on his home and his live in helpers. The truth was that Shaun

had supposed he would not be coming back, but when it came down to it, he could not bring himself to make Lewis and Lois both jobless and homeless after so many years of faithful service and besides, it would be great to have his Toronto home for summer and Christmas breaks. In the end, keeping on the Rosedale property had not been that much of a financial drain because Alicia had insisted that she certainly had sufficient funds of her own to maintain and run her home.

Shaun's kind hearted reason for not making a complete break to start his new life, had resulted in his being continually torn between two worlds.

Every time they'd flown over to stay for the summer and Christmas vacations and had had such a great time with Jonathan and Chrissy, the more he came to realise what a fish out of water he was in the UK.

He had been riding an emotional roller coaster over the past five years, really looking forward to flying home to Rosedale, enjoying practically every moment of the vacations and then suffering withdrawal symptoms immediately upon his return from which it would often take weeks to recover.

Shaun silently suffered these depressive periods and made great efforts to get close to his stepson. Anthony had also done his best to reciprocate as he carried on trying to come to terms with the tragic death of his father and the arrival, albeit several years later, of his mum's new man.

It was Bob Smart who had come to the rescue in those intervening years, dropping by several times a week to help look after and maintain Royston's classic and vintage car collection, when Anthony was home for the holidays, so it was to Bob rather than to Shaun that Anthony felt the closest.

Shaun had absolutely no interest in cars, so it would have been churlish not to have gone along with Anthony still seeing quite a lot of Bob, who by that time was quite enjoying escaping from his parental responsibilities, especially as his daughter Olivia was not the easiest of children. But again, this only served to heighten Shaun's growing sense of isolation. He had in fact become, he told himself in one of his more morose moments, a fish out of water stranded on a foreign shore.

The trouble was that he was very much the archetypal male, not being able to share his inner emotions or deepest thoughts, and Alicia was exactly the same.

She'd spent most of her twenties and early thirties being completely independent and not really interested in men. If one happened to come along, like her occasional college lecturer lover Peter, then that was OK, but if they

didn't, then that was also OK. Clearly the situation had changed when she met Royston. She was fond of him, but had she really loved him, well possibly not.
But when she and Corrine had flown out to Toronto to stay with Corinne's cousin Jonathan, there had been the out of the blue full-on holiday romance with his next door neighbour and close friend Shaun, who'd left her pregnant with Corina. She had pined for him for almost a year until his baby arrived.
Royston had never known the child wasn't his and she'd kept the secret from Shaun until after Royston's death and that fateful weekend when he and Jonathan had suddenly turned up at Luke Jameson's wedding. She'd been at a really low point for months after losing Royston, But Shaun had swept her off her feet and had come to live with her. She knew she loved him, but the trouble was that they had never really talked about their deepest and inner most feelings and now there was some invisible barrier between them. Of course, she could sense his growing unhappiness, but had not wanted to broach the subject for fear of what might follow. Then one evening, Shaun had mustered up all his emotional strength and had admitted his feelings and his desire that having spent five years living with her, perhaps it was time for the family to come and live with

him and for them to use The Woodlands as their UK holiday home.

Chapter 5

Private investigator, George Simpkins, mentally increased his fee when having driven down from London, he drew up outside the gates of The Manders, and waited to be admitted.

This former Metropolitan Police Inspector, who was middle aged, slim, handsome and smartly dressed, came highly recommended from one of Mark's city associates.

George was a hale-fellow-well-met type of character with a good ear for listening, so people often gained the impression they could tell him things in confidence which, of course, was not always the case.

The grand front door was opened to him by Frederick, The Manders elderly butler, who had been on the point of retiring, but was persuaded to stay on when Annette arrived on the scene. She'd quite liked the idea of having a butler and besides, he would be company and what Frederick did not know about the workings of the old house was not worth knowing. That she found to be particularly important during her restorations when tradesmen wanted to know how to turn the water and electricity off in various parts of the rambling old house.

Frederick was under strict instructions to bring the visitor straight up to the private study on the first floor and to hover ready to escort him off the premises because Mark fully intended this was to be a short interview, particularly as Annette and his son Mark junior were due back from their shopping expedition within the hour and there was no way he wanted her finding out what this was all about.

But once George Simpkins in his dark brown three-piece suit had settled himself comfortably into the winged arm chair opposite Mark's desk, it soon became clear that a bomb might be required to move him. To start with he spoke softly and it was almost as if his words were in no particular hurry to depart from his lips.

Mark had anticipated that once he'd given this private investigator the briefest of details, including that woman's names, nationality and the date and circumstances of her disappearance, then that would somehow be enough, but, as he quickly learned, that was not going to be nearly enough.

"Look Mark, and I hope I can call you Mark, if I am to have any possible chance of finding this Angelina Perez, or whatever she is calling herself these days, I am going to need as much background information as possible in order to build up a complete picture of her because, the

more I know about her, the more leads there will be to follow. I don't know who recommended my services, but I am certain they will have assured you that any information you give me, no matter how delicate its nature, will be treated in complete confidence.
I stand by my impeccable reputation and if I were ever to betray a confidence, the word would inevitably get out and I would be finished and I can assure you, I have absolutely no intention of being finished, because my work is my life. He paused. allowing the ticking of a grandfather clock to fill the silence.
"Now I noticed a child's trike in the hallway and that you have looked up at the clock more than once, which tells me that the lady of the house is due back shortly and that you need her knowing about this delicate matter anymore than you need a hole in the head."
Mark now feeling completely re assured, but getting more anxious by the minute at the prospect of his wife's return, was about to respond when there was a peremptory knock on the door and Annette entered the room.
"Darling, I did not know we were expecting visitors."
George was up out of his chair in an instant because he had certainly not lost the knack of moving with both speed and agility if required. "Dear lady you were not.

Allow me to introduce myself. I'm George, a very old investment friend of your husband's and I just happened to be motoring in the area when I decided, on the spur of the moment, to call in which was most rude of me." Mark could see instantly that his wife had been completely taken in and breathed an inward sigh of relief.

"Well, seeing you're here George, would you like to stay for lunch?" she asked. "Goodness no dear lady because I am due at friends in Barnstable early this afternoon, but a cup of coffee would be most appreciated. Annette said she had their son to attend to, but she'd have a pot sent up and that it was nice to have met him, albeit briefly. Once she'd left the room, George slowly lowered himself into the winged armchair and Mark looked at him with a new

respect. "That was quite a performance and I take my hat off to you, especially the line about being an old investment friend." he added. "Mark, I never go to see a potential client before checking him or her out, so now that the air has been cleared, perhaps you will kindly tell me all you know about this woman you seek."

George departed an hour later, having negotiated a substantial fee, and thinking that he might have to take himself off to Costa Rica if he ran out of leads on home territory.

Chapter 6

Architect Siegfried Summers loved his dark blue two-seater Porsche because it was a symbol of his success. It had certainly been a gamble up-rooting his busy practice from central Birmingham and downsizing to the small North Devon market town of Draymarket, but relocating to the sticks had turned out to be most fortunate. To start with people seemed to be appreciative of his talents and to have more time to discuss their requirements, which in reality, probably wasn't true, but it seemed that way. There was another reason for the move and that was his compelling need to put as much distance between himself and a particularly acrimonious divorce.

Siegfried had received a call from a Mrs Laura Jameson and was on his way to Albany House to discuss what sounded a most interesting project. She, it seemed, had got his name from her sister Corinne, who was a close friend of Alicia Randall for whom he had designed and supervised the building of a swimming pool extension. That was the thing about Draymarket, once he'd impressed a client, the bush telegraph had gone into overdrive.

Siegfried was met by Laura, Ben and Michael and was

mildly surprised to be taken into the garden of a nearby cottage and shown a faithful replica of the village, which they now wanted reproduced on a slightly larger scale. From there they walked him across to the church car park that, he was told, was going to need extending, and then through the small patch of woodland to some old red brick kennels. Siegfried agreed these had huge potential for restoration and a sensitive conversion and extension to include a small ticket office shop and café. However, he was not quite so sure they had thought through the recreation of the model village. "It seems to me there are two ways of doing this, the first being that you do increase the scale slightly and then surround the village with a circular fence, or wall, so that visitors can walk around in a clockwise direction and view it from all angles, he suggested, "And the second?" asked Ben. "The second would be to up the scale considerably to the heart of the village, including the church, the village green, your Old Mill House Visitors' Centre, The Oreford Inn and Albany House, and then to allow people to actually walk around a knee-high exact replica of their actual surroundings. Model villages were all the rage in seaside towns all over the country in the post war years, but there are few of them left now and certainly not many

like this one could be," he suggested. "That certainly is something for us to think about," Michael agreed.
Siegfried said a decision on the actual model village could wait because it would not form part of an outline planning application, the first step needed to establish that the project could go ahead, subject to a detailed application approval.
He accepted their invitation to return to Albany House for coffee and it was there the family agreed that, subject to an agreement in principle from the Church Commissioners, he could then go ahead and draw up an outline application for submission to county planners.
Draymarket Gazette Editor and Chief Reporter Jackie Benson had just returned from a singles escorted walking tour of Majorca.
This was something she'd never done before, and having enjoyed the two-week break with a dozen or so kindred spirits, it was a holiday she might well consider doing again.
Now aged 49, she regarded herself as a self-reliant single woman 'married' to her job, but there had been a certain person on the tour, with whom she had made a connection, and had agreed in a weak moment, to see again at some point over the coming months.

Arriving back in the office on that Monday morning, she was pleased to see that her deputy and former junior reporter, Ollie Banks, and their new junior, Dawn Dewsbury, fresh out of university with a first-class honour degree in English and journalism, had made quite a reasonable job of getting the paper out without her. The week prior to her departure had been particularly busy, what with the inquest on Mr Robin Lloyd of Little Oreford and the coroner's ruling that he had taken his own life while the balance of his mind had been disturbed.

"So, what's on the diary for the coming week?" she asked, having praised them for their efforts in her absence. "We've just picked up an answerphone message from the Rev Martin Clark inviting someone to pop in to his office at the vicarage later this morning because he has a terrific story for us," said Ollie.

Jackie, still a little in holiday mode, said she'd walk over to the vicarage because she hadn't seen the Rev Clark for a while and it would be nice to catch up with him.

News of Robin Lloyd's £250,000 bequest, which would remove the threat of closure that had been hanging over St Michael's in Little Oreford, was certainly a good story and would be their front page lead that week unless something better came along.

But the vicar had also mentioned something about a new model village plan. It was all under wraps at the moment, so he shouldn't really have mentioned it, but that was enough to spur Jackie on and an hour later she was popping into The Old Mill House to see Ben Jameson, who was sure to know something about this plan. He knew Jackie of old, having been pestered countless times to take advertising space in the Gazette.

But it worked both ways because she couldn't have done more to support his campaign when he was raising funds to restore the mill. "So, what brings you over here on this bright and sunny morning?" he asked. "I've just been to see Martin Clark about that most generous legacy that Robin Lloyd has left to St Michael's and he happened to mention in passing there was some plan for a new model village in Little Oreford."

Ben knew there was absolutely no point in trying to pull the wool over Jackie's eyes, and besides, they might well need the paper's support in the weeks to come. So, he told her the whole story on the understanding that she kept it to herself until the week before the planning application went in and then she'd have her scoop.

Jackie was happy to agree, but said she'd have to review the situation if the story got around and she heard about it from another source, which Ben said was fair

enough. Things were certainly on the up and up, she thought as she drove slowly back to the office.
The Gazette sales were remaining buoyant and had not suffered from the online edition she'd introduced some five years earlier having 'borrowed' some cash from the paper's trust fund to employ an online production editor. And thinking back to that, she wondered what had become of her fellow trustee Mark Hammond, who had backed her proposal, but had then resigned soon afterwards. It was then that her car phone sprang into life. "I'm missing you already," said a deep and rather distinguished voice. "Gus you can't be because it's only Monday, and three days since we all said our goodbyes at Gatwick." Jackie was not sure whether to be pleased or annoyed that he had not waited, at least a decent couple of weeks, before getting back in touch and if he hadn't, she was not sure she'd have bothered. But suddenly hearing his voice had actually surprised and pleased her because it was a very long time since anyone had showed her any attention.
Gus Masters was a dyed in the wool, Cambridge University classics fellow, with his own rooms in college and, like Jackie, had decided that he should get out more, hence his joining the walking and sightseeing tour of Majorca. They had been drawn to one another, almost

immediately, by their love of the written word, although writing for a weekly newspaper and studying classic literature could not really be further poles apart, they'd agreed. "Look Gus, although it's nice that you have called, I am just at the start of an extremely busy week, so let's catch up at the weekend," she suggested. "I am looking forward to it already," he said before ringing off. "Cheesy or what, especially for a classics scholar," she muttered.

Chapter 7

It was not long after being left Wisteria Cottage that Lottie and Andy asked Charlie how she would feel if they moved back to Little Oreford, so depriving her of her almost daily contact with her great grandchildren. "Of course, you must go and I wouldn't dream of you doing otherwise, and your idea of adopting all dear Robin and Margo's furniture as your own, rather than your mum and dad having the heartbreaking problem of clearing the cottage, is a most eminently practical solution. I know you'll need to take some essentials with you, but everything else can remain here so that you can stay over occasionally, as could Luke and Roxanne when they're back if they wished," she pointed out.

It was the following morning that Laura and Ben decided they could not put off the sad task of removing all Robin and Margo's clothing and personal effects any longer, while at the same time keeping an eye open for any documents or other evidence of what had become of Robin's love child Anna.

Laura soon came across the old photograph album that Margo had produced on that sunny morning when they'd first met on the village green and she'd been invited back for coffee, what seemed like a lifetime ago.

Kneeling on the floor in front of an open drawer, she casually turned the pages until she came upon the childhood picture of her mum with Robin and Margo and taken in the garden of Albany House. 'Mum will really treasure this,' she said to herself.
But in Robin's study, Ben was facing a far more onerous task, having opened a heavy pine cupboard to be confronted by dozens of neatly labelled boxes.
They were stuffed with literally thousands of files relating to financial and property transactions and going back literally decades. His initial inclination was to gather them all up, take them out to Robin's bonfire area, and set a match to them, because it would be very much a case of what the eye didn't see, the heart couldn't grieve. But, then again, what if some clue as to Anna's whereabouts was to go up in smoke or, more importantly, the deeds to the cottage!
Luckily, a quick call to Eustace established that the cottage deeds were lodged in his possession, as were all the other legal documents relating to the Lloyds' property and important financial transactions. So, all those boxes need not receive more than a cursory glance, he was assured, still even that was going to be easier said than done.
They went home for a quick lunch and it was late

afternoon and getting dark outside when Ben at last came across a small box tucked away behind one of the much larger ones at the bottom of the cupboard, probably in a place where Margo would never have found it. Laura had already gone back to begin preparing supper when Ben drew out, what was actually and old shoebox, and carefully removed its lid to discover a bundle of letters tied around with string which he carefully undid. They were indeed love letters from Rachael, as he'd hardly dared to have hoped, but clearly written in the early days of their heady relationship when they were actually living together. They were simply addressed 'from my side of the bed, which was really quite bizarre, and were of such a graphically sexual nature, that Ben felt almost too embarrassed to do other than scan through them and decide he would definitely not be showing them to Laura.
But the last letter was in a yellowing envelope and addressed to Robin at his old London home. Drawing it carefully out and slowly unfolding it, Ben was intensely aware that Robin would have been the last person to have set eyes on it, a lifetime ago. It was headed New Grimsby House, Glastonbury, Somerset, September 1974 and had been written with a fountain pen in a bold,

but rounded script that was surprisingly easy to read, even though the blue ink had faded.

'My dearest Robin, I thought I would drop you this short note to let you know that Anna and I are both well and are currently staying with a close relation in Glastonbury. Our daughter has settled in well at the junior school and is showing a clear talent for drawing and painting. I think this must come from my father's side of the family, because I had a great uncle, who was a fine portrait painter, unless, of course there were artists in your family. Please, please, do not attempt to contact me because our personalities are such that it would surely only lead to more emotional fireworks and that would definitely not be good for Anna. But I promise I will write to you from time to time to let you know how we are getting along. All my love for now, Rachael xxx, Ben decided that he'd done quite enough for one day and took the letter home to show Laura.

"Rachael can't have kept her promise because this is the only letter and I'm sure he would have kept others if he had received them," said Ben. They decided over supper that they would make a trip to Glastonbury and try to find out what had become of Rachael and Anna, but that would take several days, so they would leave it for the time being.

All further thoughts of looking for Anna were kicked further down the road the following morning while Ben was watching over a blazing bonfire in the back garden of Wisteria Cottage and his mobile phone rang in his pocket. It was Jackie Benson.

"Hi Ben, I know it's only a couple of days since I saw you, but believe it or not, word of your new model village proposal has actually got out," she told him. "Really! So how do you know?" Ben challenged. "Well, I've just put the phone down on, Fred Mullins, Chairman of the Little Oreford Allotments Association, saying he'd heard a rumour about the old kennels site being turned into a model village. I could tell he was really hot under the collar, saying that if it turned out to be true, then he and his fellow allotment holders would fight the plan tooth and nail because it would completely shatter their peace and quiet."

Ben turned and walked away from the fire, which had luckily started dying down after the initial conflagration, and settled himself on the nearest garden seat.

"Jackie did Fred say where this rumour had come from?" he asked. "Yes, apparently, it was his daughter who told him. She'd heard it while waiting to pick her children up from Hampton Green Primary," Jackie explained. Then the penny dropped.

‘Oh! so that’s how it possibly got out because Lottie would also have been waiting outside the school to pick up his own grandchildren, Jack and Hannah, and might well have mentioned it in conversation, he reasoned. But that would not have been her fault because, come to think of it, neither she nor Andy had been at the Sunday morning meeting with the Rev Clark, when it was agreed to keep the whole thing under wraps, but even then, he’d let it slip in an unguarded moment.

“I see Jackie, so what do you propose doing about investigating this rumour because, even Fred has described it as simply being a rumour,” he asked, neatly tossing this hot potato back into her lap. There was a pause while Jackie considered the question. “Yes Ben, but the trouble is that you and I both know that it’s not just a rumour, don’t we? she pointed out. “OK,” said Ben. “I assume you’ll be running the great news story about Robin Lloyd’s £250,000 bequest to save St Michael’s from the threat of closure in this week’s paper,” he said, thinking aloud. “Yes. It’s actually going to be tomorrow’s front-page lead,” replied Jackie.

“That being the case, and as the kennels are actually on church land, and it was the Rev Clark himself, who told you about the model village idea, give me a few days and I’ll discuss it with the vicar to see if we can come up with a joint statement," he suggested. "All right Ben, that does sound like a plan, so I'll do nothing until I hear from you," promised Jackie.

Ben played the hose on the now smouldering mound of paper to make sure the fire was well and truly out and to prevent any scraps being blown away, before locking up the cottage and strolling thoughtfully across the green back to his office.

There was no need to bring Lottie into this now, even if she'd unwittingly happened to mention the plan, because it was the vicar himself who'd let the cat out of the bag, he reasoned.

Once back behind his desk, he called Corinne, who was luckily on reception, and asked if she could pop over to the house, say just after six, and if Michael happened to be around then, perhaps he could come too, because something had come up.

"So, what are we going to do now?" Michael asked, after Ben had explained just what had happened. "I feel rather guilty because this whole model village idea was mine and it already appears to have opened a can of worms," he admitted. "You were dead right, Corinne, when you said the allotment people would get upset," he conceded. "It was, and still is, a good idea Michael," said Ben. "And don't forget, that the vicar was well up for it,

and if it hadn't been for his enthusiasm, then I don't think we'd have jumped in quite so quickly and got an architect involved," he added. "So where are we going from here?" asked Laura. "I think we should now ditch the idea of converting the old kennels into a visitors' centre," replied Ben. "Luckily there's plenty of room for everything, including a small wooden café building, completely out of sight on the far side of the plot, and that would probably be cheaper than messing around with the old building anyway," he pointed out.
"Tomorrow, Robin's bequest to St Michael's and how it's going to save our church from any threat of closure for years to come, is going to be front page news in the Gazette," Ben told them.
"So, with the Rev Clark's support, I suggest we put out a joint statement for next week's paper, saying that, as lasting tribute to Robin Lloyd's generosity, we would like to replicate the wonderful model village he has created in his garden, on a larger site for everyone to share. But that the old kennels, opposite the allotments, would be left untouched. We could also stage an Open Day and invite everyone in the village to visit Wisteria Cottage's garden to see Robin's creation, and just think what great PR for the project that would be," Ben pointed out.

"Bloody hell, Ben, I really believe this might work in generating a huge amount of tacit local support for when we do submit that outline planning application," said Michael.

The Rev Clark, still inspired by his vision of seeing St Michael's centre stage in the village after so many years of decline and neglect, was only too pleased to support the statement.

He'd already been in touch with the Church Commissioners and had received a cautious, but not discouraging response.

Jackie Benson was delighted because she now had a great follow-up story for next week's paper, if not the lead, if nothing more interesting came along. She knew this could run and run as she kept her readers updated on the progress of the project.

The Little Oreford model village proposal did make the following week's lead and had included an invitation to readers to come along to an Open Day viewing of Robin's model village.

Ben and Laura reckoned that well over one hundred local people had turned up during that busy day, many with young families, and the overall impression they'd gained was one of general support.

Chapter 8

Anthony Randall always really looked forward to the family's summer and Christmas business class flights with Air Canada from London to Toronto. In the summer there was so much to look forward to, including extended visits to Jonathan's lakeside camp, where he'd learned to paddle a canoe, fish and make campfires in the woods, and also to have his first faltering attempts at water skiing. Then at Christmas there were all Toronto's spectacular festive events to attend, plus the big Christmas lunch that Lois and Lewis prepared for them all, including Jonathan and Chrissy and their now four-year-old daughter Sophia. There was always a huge tree and masses of presents and everyone was in a fun mood, especially when, late on Christmas afternoon, they divided into teams and played charades. Last year he'd played with Lewis and, to everyone's surprise, they'd won easily, so hopefully he could partner with him Then there was the chance that it would snow, which never ever happened in Devon at Christmas, but could happen in Toronto, even though, being on Lake Ontario, the climate was milder than most other parts of the country.

Last, they'd woken up to a white Christmas and that had been brilliant because Jonathan had a toboggan and an old pair of skis and they'd driven out to the nearest ski resort between Christmas and the New Year and he'd had a great time.
His stepdad was always in such a good mood when they were at his house, but that was not always the case at home and he now knew, or thought he knew, the reason why.
It was one evening last month when Corinne and Michael had been over for supper and he'd come down to the kitchen for a glass of water. As he'd approached the door, he'd heard mum and Corinne talking and it was something about the way that they were talking that had made him stop and listen. Then he'd heard how his stepdad wanted them all to move over to Toronto, but that Mum didn't really want to go because of him and the effect it would have on his life. He'd turned around and gone back up to his room, but could not stop thinking about the conversation and it had been playing on his mind ever since, because, rather than being afraid that it would happen, he'd actually begun to hope that it might.
To start with, him and Michael, who had been inseparable best friends since junior school days, were going to be parted in the New Year.

His parents were moving to Scotland and had decided he should leave Camleigh College, so he was not looking forward to that. Not having to go to boarding school anymore and being able to spend loads more time up at Jonathan's camp would be absolutely great. But if mum insisted on his staying at Camleigh, then why couldn't he just spend the odd weekend with Corinne and Michael and fly back over to Toronto for all his holidays, as long as he could always fly business class, that was!

Anthony got his wish and he did partner Lewis again for charades on Christmas afternoon, but although it had been a close-run thing it was mum and Chrissy who'd won with dad, Corina, Sophia and Jonathan coming last. Then it popped into his head that after another week all the fun and festivities would be over and they'd be packing their bags and flying home again.

Suddenly, the idea of actually moving to Canada was back on his mind and wouldn't go away.

It was on a cold and sunny afternoon, a couple of days later, when they'd all taken the short ferry ride over to Ward's Island and were walking close to the lake shore with magnificent views of the city skyline across the water, that Anthony finally decided to broach the subject.

Jonathan and Chrissy were in front with Corina holding little Sophia's hand and he was walking some yards behind with mum and Shaun. "Mum and Dad, can I ask you both a question that's been on my mind for quite a while now?" he said. "Of course, you can darling," Alicia responded. "Go on then son," added Shaun, pleased that Anthony had called him 'dad,' which didn't happen very often. He hesitated. "Well, when the summer comes, instead of just flying over for our holidays, why can't we all come and live here and not go home again. The suggestion. coming out of a crystal clear blue Canadian sky, just hung there in the crisp cold air for a few seconds as both Alicia and Shaun grappled to absorb the personal enormity of it. Shaun instinctively held back waiting for Alicia's response. "That would be quite a move, but what about your schooling darling? You're so close to your exams now," she pointed out. "Yes, but I'll be taking those before the summer, so that doesn't matter, and I'm going off the whole idea of boarding now that Michael isn't going to be there anymore." Still Shaun held back from saying anything, but then Anthony put him on the spot. "What do you think Dad? Do you think it would be a good idea?" he asked.

"If your mum and you would be happy then, of course, I would be very happy too." It was a clever response. "So, shall we, Mum?
Shall we come over in the summer and not go home, except for Christmas and summer holidays, like we do here, but in reverse?" It was a fait accompli and Alicia knew it. If that really was what Anthony now wanted, and there was no question, as far as Shaun was concerned, then how could she resist any further. "This will take some thinking about and a lot of organising, but if, at the end of the day, it's still what the two most important men in my life really want, then I suppose my answer must be 'yes.' Suddenly Shaun saw a whole new world of possibilities opening up and he owed it all to his stepson. So maybe they could find a place by the lake shore to establish their own summer camp, or maybe all go off family camping in the spring. Then on a practical front, he had several new business ventures in mind, which had all been put on hold when he'd moved to the UK, but could now be taken out of the drawer in the recesses of his creative mind and dusted off again. Anthony, elated that he'd so easily persuaded his mum, suddenly ran ahead to join the others. But then Shaun, who was at heart very much a kind and considerate man, started feeling guilty that he would be tearing Alicia

away from her whole way of life just to satisfy his desires. "We don't really have to do this you know, because I do really love you and if it would make you so terribly unhappy, then what would be the point?" he asked. suddenly taking her hand and squeezing it. "Yes, we do my love because, as you so rightly told me, it's your turn now.

But I do wish Anthony had come out with all of this before I splashed all that cash on the pool extension. It was a joke and he knew it. "But beginning to talk practically for a moment, what are you going to do about Lewis and Lois, because, while on the one hand, I really wouldn't want them living with us, I also wouldn't be happy to see them lose their grand home after so many years?" she told him. "I can't say that I haven't already been thinking about that and my conclusion was that I could, find them somewhere else to live and that they could both come around and help you out a couple of days a week, if they wanted, because it's a big place to manage, especially outside."

But more importantly, would you want to keep The Woodlands as our holiday home, because it's a big place with a lot of ground and it hasn't got a live-in Lewis and Lois to look after it. Alicia knew instantly there was no way she was ever going to give up the home that she and Royston had shared, even if it meant finding a Lewis and Lois of her own to look after it. Besides that, what would become of his beloved car collection which Anthony would never countenance her selling off?

It had been arranged that they'd be going back to Jonathan and Chrissy's for supper, so that would give them the perfect opportunity to break their news.

Chapter 9

Back home in Little Oreford, it had been a horrendously busy festive season with everyone working flat out at The Oreford Inn and The Cheringford Arms, with both hostelries being fully booked for pre-Christmas lunches and suppers, and all the accommodation taken between Christmas and over the New Year.

Life had been made easier for Andy because, he and Lottie and the twins, had moved into Wisteria Cottage at the beginning of December, so he now only needed to walk across the village green to his frenetically busy kitchen, and could also find the odd moment to pop home for a brief respite. But it had definitely not been so easy for Corinne and Michael. She had been living, mostly in her apartment, and running the inn, while he was totally absorbed, managing The Cheringford, while overseeing its kitchen operation, and then driving the few miles down the road to his, still rented, place in Wixton to grab a few hours' sleep.

He'd appointed a trainee Deputy Manager in good time for the festive season, The young lady had shown much early promise, having been a star student at his former county catering college. But suddenly, after a few busy, and quite stressful, days, she decided that a career in catering and hospitality management was not for her and had resigned and left him in the lurch. Getting their work-life balance in perspective had got to be their priority early in the New Year, they'd decided. But, in the meantime, they had a holiday in the Canary Islands booked for the last week in January when both coaching inns would still be closed to give everyone a short break.

Alicia, Shaun and the family had been back home for a couple of days when she called Corinne and invited herself over to The Oreford for a catch up and because she had something important to share with her.

"OK, so what's this important news then?" Corinne, asked once the coffee had been poured. Alicia took a deep breath.

"We're all moving over to Toronto in August, after Anthony's finished his exams, and then living life in reverse by flying back to The Woodlands for our family Christmas and summer breaks. But while I know I'm going to miss you all, terribly, I will be coming back by myself at least four other times a year."

Corinne put down her mug in surprise. "Whatever changed your mind, especially when you had such misgivings about the effect on Anthony?" she asked.

"Actually, it was Anthony, who decided he really wanted to move to Toronto," said Alicia, explaining what had happened when they were all out on a family walk around the lake shore. "I know I had a lot of misgivings, but now I'm quite looking forward to the dramatic change in our lives, and also to having the promised freedom to come and go as I please, she explained. "So, who's going to be looking after The Woodlands while you're not around, because I don't suppose you're going to want to leave it completely unattended?"

Alicia paused. "Well, I do have an idea, but I need to know what you think about it before I take it any further, because if you don't think it's a good idea, then I'll be trying to work something else out," she explained. "This sounds intriguing, so go on, do tell," said Corinne. "I'm wondering whether Bob and Annie would like to move in with Olivia and treat the place as their own.

They could live rent and bills free in exchange for just being there and keeping an eye on things. Bob, as you know, has been over regularly to help Anthony with all the cars, ever since I lost Royston, and Annie often comes over with Olivia, so it seemed like the perfect solution if they were up for it." She hesitated.

"But of course, like everything, there would be knock-on consequences because they do a lot for your mum and I know how particularly close Annie is to her. I don't think they'd really want to leave her all on her own at Little

Oreford Court, especially now that Lottie and Andy and the twins have moved into the village. So, what shall I do Corinne? Should I ask them and put them in a dilemma, because it's your mum who's going to be the one losing out and there's no way I am going to do anything to upset you and Laura."

Corinne picked up the coffee pot and gave them both a refill.

"Now that is something to think about and, to tell you the truth, Laura and I have been vaguely wondering what is going to be happening to mum longer term, now that she's in her eighties.

I think we'd just assumed she'd be staying put with the help of a team of privately employed carers, as and when they were needed. Mum has a will of her own, as you well know, and will do exactly whatever she wants to do. But I know she's missing having the twins popping in and out, whenever they felt like it, and may now be feeling just a bit left out on her own over at Little Oreford. So, to lose Annie and Bob as well, would be a real blow," she admitted. "That settles it then because there's no way I'm going to put them or you and Laura in such a dilemma," declared Alicia.

"Hang on a minute, because having mum back here in Little Oreford, where she'd be completely free to go walk

about and see us all without having to rely on being taken everywhere, might well be the answer. So, before you do anything else, let me discuss this with Laura and Ben and if we can come up with a plan, then we could ask mum what she thinks. Who knows, she might be quite happy to moving back into the village, and if so, you could go ahead and ask Bob and Annie.
Anyway, how are Jonathan, Chrissy and little Sophia because it sounds like you all had a wonderful time together?"
Alicia thought for a moment there was just the slightest hint that her best friend might be wondering how life might have turned out if she and Jonathan had stayed together. She suddenly realised just how cruel it would be if she said how blissfully happy they all seemed. But Corinne did not give her a chance to answer. "That's the thing, you see, because when it came to it, Shaun was ready to give up everything and move over here to be with you and now you are giving up everything to go and live in Toronto. Neither Jonathan nor I could ever have contemplated doing that, so I guess our relationship, as good as it was, was doomed to failure in the end," A sadness had stolen over Corinne's face as she glimpsed how things might have been.

"But everything worked out well in the end, because you and Michael are happy, aren't you?" she asked. "Yes, we are, but we've been so busy over Christmas and New Year that we've been a bit like the proverbial ships passing in the night," she admitted.
"Look, you've told me you're off to The Canaries next week, so you and Michael will have some time to really think about just how you want your lives to be going forward," Corinne smiled at the thought of their fast approaching respite in the sun. "It's already top of the agenda," she replied.
Alicia stayed for a spot of lunch and when she'd gone, Corinne walked over to Albany House to share her news with Laura and with Ben, who was about to walk back over to The Old Mill House. Her sister was the firsts to respond. "Of course, it will be mum's decision, but surely, she'd be better off here where she can easily see everyone rather than being stuck out at Little Oreford Court," she pointed out. Ben immediately began thinking about what they might do with Little Oreford Court if it became vacant. "So how about we convert the upper floor of the Old Mill House into a spacious new apartment for her with a lift to her own entrance on the ground floor," he suggested.

Corrine and Laura agreed that might well be the answer and decided there would be nothing to lose from driving over and finding out what Charlie actually thought about the prospect.

"This is a surprise, seeing both my girls together, so what can possibly have happened to have afforded me this unexpected pleasure?" asked Charlie, with a twinkle in her eye.

"That certainly is something for me to think about," she agreed, once she' heard what her daughters had to say. "I can appreciate Alicia is going to need an answer, but obviously not in that much of a hurry, seeing they'll not actually be moving over there until the summer."

When her girls had gone, Charlie, still sitting in her favourite armchair, beside her recently lit log fire on that cold winter's afternoon, began wondering what she really did think about moving back into the village. It would mean swopping her comfortable home with all her favourite things around her, for a brand-new apartment, and the answer, she decided, was 'no.'

She really would miss Annie and Bob and little Olivia, and the comfort of knowing they were just a few steps away. It was also a great help that Bob was always willing to run her into the village or Draymarket in the dear old Bentley. But no, she would not stand in their

way if they wanted to accept Alicia's invitation.
'Yes, that dear old Bentley,' she thought, suddenly transported back to that never to be forgotten day when she, Bob and Annie left the Atlantic View retirement hotel in Sidmouth and made their way back to Little Oreford, only to find her precious, long lost, but never forgotten, girls.
The latest edition of the Draymarket Gazette, which had been on her lap ready to open, slipped to the floor and she was asleep.

Chapter 10

Private investigator, George Simpkins, had just brought his latest case to a profitable conclusion and had jetted off down to Niece after New Year for a few days, staying at his favourite hotel, going for long walks along the Promenade des anglais and spending a couple of evenings in his favourite casino.

He was a man, who enjoyed a routine when he was not on a case, and had become a familiar figure with the hotel concierge and front desk teams, the patron of his favourite restaurant and, of course, the always friendly and welcoming cashiers and croupiers at the casino where he sometimes enjoyed a little success. George spoke French fluently. He enjoyed being made welcome and being able to ask after a son or a grandchild, while being served by Dominic, the patron of his favourite restaurant. This was in complete contrast to the other side of his life where he did not want people having the slightest clue as to who he was or about his business in hand.

It had been a particularly enjoyable break, especially the couple of evening and nights he'd spent with Antoinette, his regular escort on these occasions, George mused as he drove his nondescript saloon up the slip road, onto

the busy M4, and joined the steady stream of traffic heading out of London.
He was on his way to the market town of Draymarket, in North Devon and had booked into a chain hotel because, annoyingly, the inn at Little Oreford, where Angelina Perez, or whatever she was calling herself these days, had last been seen attending a local wedding, was closed.
George always enjoyed doing the background legwork for a new assignment and was looking forward to spending a couple of, all expenses paid, days wandering around Draymarket and Little Oreford, and where ever else his inquiries might lead.
Following up on the wedding, although it had been in October five years earlier, was the obvious place to start. So, after checking in at the hotel, he strolled up the Draymarket High Street to get his bearings and called in at The Carpenters Arms for a pint and a spot of lunch before making his way over to Little Oreford. Not being able to stay at the village inn was a bit of a pain, but no matter, he would start by visiting the parish church where the wedding had been and take it from there.
George had received a call from his client, seeking a progress report, the previous week and had politely confirmed that he was about to start work, because his

earlier case had run on slightly longer than anticipated. That was a lie because the truth was that there was no way he was going to embark on a fresh investigation until he enjoyed his well-earned break.

But now he was back in harness and was hoping for some lucky break, which could happen when one started covering new ground on case.

A steady drizzle was falling as he parked up beside the Little Oreford village green, fished a black brolly out of his boot, and walked across to the church, which luckily, he found open.

Not much stuff must get nicked in this quiet backwater he supposed. George entered St Michael's and looked around before posting thirty pence for the latest edition of the parish magazine into an old wooden honesty box. Retiring to one of the pews at the back of the church to read it, he soon learned that St Michael's had been saved from closure, thanks to a most generous £250,000 donation from the late Robin Lloyd, while a previous donation of £30,000 had been made by a local businessman, some five years earlier. 'That might prove useful, seeing that the wedding, in which he was interested, had taken place in the October of that year,' he mused. 'So, locals, reading this article, might also remember the wedding, which, according to his client, had been lavish and the local equivalent of a society affair,' he concluded.

George took out the small notebook and pencil, he always kept in an inside jacket pocket, and noted down the names and telephone numbers of the vicar and the two church wardens, whose contact details he'd spotted in the back of the magazine. So, what was to stop him driving back into town, seeking out the vicar, the Rev Martin Clark, and offering to make his own 'modest' donation, which again could be put on expenses.

That, George decided, was indeed a plan, which could be executed immediately and was probably best carried out without phoning for an appointment, which might easily result in a delay. It did not really matter if the vicar was not at home, seeing he was staying close by anyway, and could easily pop back again in the morning.

As it happened, the Rev Clark, was at home and the mere mention of a donation for St Michael's was enough to propel George into a comfortable armchair in the vicar's study.

"As I was saying vicar, I was really impressed by St Michael's, and particularly that early stained glass window above the altar. He paused for effect.

"So, I was thinking that I might also offer a donation.

But clearly not along the lines of the most generous ones I read about in your parish magazine." Martin assured him that any donation, however small, would be most gratefully received and that 'yes' £250 would indeed be most welcome and that, of course, he could wait for a cheque posted to him in due course.
He did not have even the slightest doubt that the donation from this most generous stranger would be forthcoming and asked George if he had time to stay for a cup of tea and a slice of his home-made fruit cake. George said that, of course, he had time for a cuppa and, as it happened, he too was a dab hand when it came to baking cakes.
"As you say, vicar, declining congregations are becoming a worrying feature of churches in small villages all over the country and I guess St Michael's is no exception. I suppose that must also apply to a shrinking number of weddings," he remarked.
"Yes, you are absolutely right and I guess it's some five years since we had a big wedding at St Michael's," Martin obligingly replied. This was sweet music to George's ears. It was as if this unsuspecting country vicar was a large trout that could not wait to jump on to his well baited hook. "That sounds like it was big affair for you to remember it so well," he probed. "Yes. It was

the Jamesons' son. They're the family who run The Oreford Inn and the village's Old Mill House Heritage Centre and Craft Workshops."

Now, that's a most promising start,' George said to himself, having made his excuses and left, and was walking thoughtfully back to his hotel.

"All he needed to do now was to find some unsuspecting local guest, who might, actually, have come across Angelina during the course of the wedding. She was a strikingly handsome woman, he could see from the picture Mark Hammond had given him, and would stand out in any crowd, so that was definitely an advantage. There was, he later discovered, a small Italian bistro in the High Street and he was particularly fond of Italian cuisine. But with only one other couple dining, that didn't hold out too much hope for a good experience, although in the end, he was pleasantly surprised. Further up the street, he came upon a small convenience store and popped in for a Times. He also picked up a copy of the weekly Draymarket Gazette, which might definitely be worth a trawl through, he thought, as he crossed over to The Carpenters Arms. The pub was quiet, it being a Monday evening, so George ordered a small brandy and settled down to tackle The Times crossword and to see what the Gazette had to offer and, yes, it did have something to offer. There on the front page was the story of how the residents of Little Oreford had flocked to Wisteria Cottage to see the late Mr Robin Lloyd's much loved model village. As a result of this open day success, the Jameson family were submitting an outline planning application for the creation of a replica village on a much larger scale on a small plot of land beyond the parish church, he read.

The piece was accompanied by a picture of a Ben Jameson, Director of The Old Mill House Heritage Centre and the Rev Martin Clark, standing together on the proposed site.

The vicar, it seemed, was very much in favour of the project, which might attract more visitors to St Michael's. The story concluded by saying the original idea had been to restore and incorporate the long abandoned Little Oreford Hunt kennels, but this had been dropped because it was close to the village allotments, whose members' peace might have been disturbed. These Jamesons were clearly an influential family, so perhaps a visit to The Old Mill House Heritage Centre, might just bring him a little closer to discovering what had become of their highly attractive Costa Rican wedding guest, he decided.

George got up late and only just made it into the hotel's

nearby chain restaurant for breakfast, so it was getting on for eleven when he strolled into the Heritage Centre to find it surprisingly busy, seeing how early it was in the New Year. All these visitors must have been the occupants of a coach he'd noticed drawn up outside and this was fortunate because it meant he could look around without drawing attention to himself.

There appeared to be seven or eight craft workshops, the largest of which was a silversmiths called Fortune and Bright, which occurred to George as most amusing given their trade.

They most likely made engagement and wedding rings and as it was a certain wedding he was interested in, then this was clearly a good place to start. George ambled in and began looking casually into the various show cases displaying their wares, while at the same time catching the unmistakable bitter smell of some soldering work going on behind the closed workshop door.

"Can I be of any assistance?" Turning, he saw an aproned and whiskered man with a round face and an open friendly smile, who could not have been more than five foot tall.

"Hello, are you Mr Fortune or Mr Bright, might I ask?" responded George returning the engaging smile.

"I'm Mr Bright. Mr Fortune is having a couple of days off because he was in over the weekend," he explained. "Do you alternate?" asked George, quickly picking up the vibe that this was a man, who'd be up for a bit of banter.
"No not really, because he's single and doesn't mind working weekends, while I have a family and they definitely do mind," replied Mr Bright.
"Then you really do have an arrangement that suits you both," said George. He'd made up his mind that he really liked Mr Bright and was going to commission a gold ring as a present to himself from his recent winnings at the casino.
Thirty minutes later, spurred on by a commission worth several hundred pounds, Charles Bright had invited George into his workshop for coffee in giant mugs, made in the pottery next door. Not unsurprisingly, the conversation got around to weddings, and one wedding in particular. "Yes, that was certainly a most memorable occasion. Everyone who works here got invited and we all contributed an item we'd made as a combined wedding gift for the couple," recalled Charles. "There were so many guests they had to use part of the village green as an overspill car park." Now George was ready to pounce, because if that vicar had been a big fat trout, then Mr Bright could only be described as a rather plump

mouse. "Quite by chance, a Costa Rican woman friend of mine was also at the wedding, so I don't suppose you came across her by any chance, did you?" George asked innocently. "Oh yes. She was a real stunner and our party were on a table quite close by, so I could hardly not have noticed her," he said.
"That is a coincidence then, because I haven't seen her since," said George, wondering if his stroke of luck on the roulette wheel was about to roll on. "I'm not surprised, because she went off to Toronto with a Canadian called Jonathan Meyer, who's related to the Jamesons, and ended up marrying him." Could this really be happening? George asked himself. "How do you know all that?" he questioned. "Oh! this place is a real gossip factory because most of us have lived and worked together for years."
It was if that tiny white roulette ball had just rolled into George's lucky number nine slot.
Job done and that was going to the easiest £3000 fee he'd ever earned, George thought as he said goodbye to the most obliging Charles Bright, having paid in advance for his ring and given him a box numbered address for its delivery.
This whole Jameson family set-up intrigued him and he suddenly had an overwhelming desire to make Ben

Jameson's acquaintance and to go and see this famous model village for himself. Spotting a door grandly marked 'Heritage Director,' he found himself tapping gently on it. Ben had just returned from lunch and called out to whoever it was to 'come in.'
George slowly opened the door and put his head cautiously around it. "Do come in," invited Ben, seeing at a glance that George in his smart three-piece suit was by no means his average visitor. "So how can I help you?" he asked, gesturing George to the seat on the opposite side of his cluttered desk.
"I'm down from London and on my way to see a potential client in Barnstable, but decided to stop off in Draymarket last night.
I happened to pick up a copy of your local paper and read all about your model village plan. It intrigued me because there's a splendid one in Beaconsfield, near High Wycombe, where I grew up. I spent quite a bit of my childhood in there, so I was wondering if there was any chance that I might take a look at your one, seeing that I'm here." It was true, George had grown up near Beaconsfield, but had never shown even the slightest interest in its model village. His story sounded convincing because Ben, Laura and the kids had also visited the Beaconsfield attraction, while on a family

camping holiday the Chilterns, "I'm afraid the late Robin Lloyd's village is on a far smaller scale, which you may well find disappointing, but we do intend to recreating a larger version, if we are granted permission. Having said that, I do have some time to spare, so I could take you over to see it if you like." George said he'd like that very much and would love to take a look, if the Heritage Director was sure he really did have the time to spare.
"So might I ask what business brings you down this way?" Ben asked conversationally, after they had visited Wisteria Cottage and had emerged back on to the village green. "I am a retired policeman and now private investigator," George replied.
He would not normally have revealed his occupation, unless it was necessary, but some perverse quality in his nature took hold. He was delighting in the fact that he had come down to this quiet Devon backwater and had achieved his ultimate goal, while pulling the proverbial wool over everyone's eyes.
"That's quite extraordinary because my family and I may well be in need of a man with your talents, come to think of it.
So do you have some time to discuss it now, or should you be getting over to Barnstable?" George said he had plenty of time and before he knew it, he found himself

sitting down for a cuppa with Ben and Laura in Albany House, which was probably the nerve centre of this most interesting family enterprise.

"Being a private investigator must be most interesting Mr Simpkins," said Laura, while pouring the tea at their kitchen table. "To tell you the truth, Mrs Jameson, it's not really," replied George, now secretly delighted at having yet another amazing stroke of luck. "I spend an awful lot of my time on behalf of parents, who have lost touch with their grown-up children, for one reason or another, often after some family bust-up.

Then, if I do find them, the chances are they do not want to get back in touch anyway," he explained. "At least then you can give your clients the peace of mind of knowing they're all right," said Laura brightly. "I suppose there is that," admitted George, who'd actually long since given up taking such commissions.

"So, Mr Simpkins, might you now be willing to spend some of your valuable time on a similar case that we have in mind?" asked Ben. "Please do tell me how I might assist," invited George, drawing out his notebook from an inner pocket.

"There's not really a lot to go on, other than it was Robin's last wish that we should try and find out what had become of his long-lost daughter, whose last known address was the Somerset pop festival town of Glastonbury some thirty years ago?" explained Ben.

"This really does sound like my sort of case, especially as Mr Lloyd was the creator of your model village, so I would be delighted to assist," said George. "Do you have any other information, which might help me in my enquiries?"

Ben got up from the table and soon returned with the last letter that Rachael had written to Robin from Glastonbury and handed it to him. "Now do tell me all that you can about her?" George invited. They related all they could remember from that momentous afternoon when Robin's will was read.

"So what about your fee, Mr Simpkins?" asked Laura.

"To start with, I think the time has come for you call me George.

"And as for my charges, I will naturally expect you to pay all my fully receipted hotel and other expenses, while I am staying in Glastonbury, and where ever else this search should take me."

He paused to cleared an annoying tickle in his throat.

"As far as my £3000 fee is concerned, shall we say I take this commission on a no win no fee basis, other than perhaps a nominal £500 for my trouble." Laura and Ben looked at one another in surprise. "That's most

generous of you George, but are you completely sure you want to do that?" Laura asked.
"Yes, Mrs Jameson, because I do enjoy a challenge, and in this way, I have a real incentive to succeed don't you see."
Mark Hammond was not best pleased at having to fork out £3000, plus expenses, for a commission that had clearly taken this private investigator only a few days to fulfil. Still, he had been warned that while George Simpkins was extremely good at what he did, he was expensive and the fact that with a little further research, he had actually come up with the address and contact details for Joseph B Meyer and Sons lawyers of University Avenue, Toronto, was indeed proof of that. But to hear that his former girlfriend, who'd jilted him at that bloody wedding, had married this clearly wealthy lawyer, irked him no end.
Still there would be some consolation if she was now in serious trouble with her former employers.
It was late afternoon in San Jose when Senior Serious Crime Officer Carlos Diaz picked up the call from Mark Hammond, giving him pretty much the exact whereabouts of his former operative Chrissy Morales, who had simply dropped off his radar. Carlos felt during their early years together working to bring down the

Jimarenal Corporation, they had become confidants, although she had always strictly maintained her professional distance. He was reasonably happily married with two daughters, but if she had come on to him, he was not sure he could have resisted her, but that had never happened so he was spared the temptation. Chrissy had always been fanatical about keeping her personal life totally to herself, so much so, that in the early days her colleagues had even thought about trailing her.

It was Carlos' total commitment to bringing down the corrupt corporation that had eventually triumphed. Then, flushed with success, and in search of more recognition, he'd decided to go after Mark Hammond and the hedge fund, he'd probably launched with the millions of dollars of drug money which the corporation had poured into it. He could not believe that Mark had not been a party to this massive international money laundering operation. That was why he'd trusted Chrissy with the task of flying to Zurich, under the alias Angelina Perez, to see if she could discover any hard evidence to back up his belief. For the first few months, all had seemed to be going remarkably well. Chrissy, like the true professional she was, had easily worked her way into this man's confidence, having the free run of his penthouse HQ and even being set up in her own apartment.

But the last he'd heard from her was to say she was flying to his home in England to attend a wedding and that was five years ago. Not long after that, Carlos had become heavily involved in another major long-running corruption case. Then his marriage had fallen apart, so all thoughts of finding out what had happened to Chrissy had slipped further and further down his ever-growing list of priorities.

That woman certainly knew how to look after herself, so he doubted she would have come to any serious harm, he'd always rationalised. But now he found himself in the unusual position of having some time on his hands and the desire to know what had become of his former operative, suddenly became uppermost in his mind. He'd certainly given up a long time ago on the self-seeking, glory hunting, need to prove that Mark Hammond had knowingly accepted the Jimarenal Corporation's money. But this meant he'd sent a woman, he'd respected and trusted, over to Europe on a fruitless mission, from which she'd never returned. So, with all that on his mind, he'd sent for the large bundle of Jimarenal Corporation files and eventually pulled out the notes on her final call to him, which included the address and telephone number of The Manders. A quick search told him it was just after 9am in the UK, so a reasonable time to see if he could get hold of this Mark Hammond, who'd picked up the phone. Now, three weeks later, he'd just called Carlos back with the surprising news that Chrissy had met a lawyer called Jonathan Meyer at the wedding and had flown back to Toronto where she'd married him.

Carlos put the phone down and sat back behind the large, colonial style, wooden desk that Chrissy and her colleagues had struggled to carry up from the ground floor on that memorable day he'd had taken over the department, and wondered what to do next. The story had a happy ending, so he could finally stop worrying about what had become of Chrissy Morales, but perhaps it might be good to call her up at some point, at least for old time's sake, he decided.

Chapter 11

Corinne breathed a sigh of relief as she and Michael finally belted themselves into their seats in the A320 Airbus standing on the tarmac at Bristol International Airport and bound for Fuerteventura in the Canary Islands. It had been a frantic few weeks, but now, hopefully, they could relax and just enjoy a complete rest in the sun. The previous afternoon, instead of starting to pack, she and Laura had received a call from Charlie asking them to pop over to discuss her future.
Her mum had made it clear, that although she appreciated that they'd create a lovely new apartment for her in the Old Mill House, she was going to stay in her own home and would not stand in Bob and Annie's way, if they did decide to take up Alicia's offer. Lottie was still bringing Jack and Hannah in to see her most days, and she was sure that Bob and Annie would be calling in regularly with little Olivia, and even have her over to tea at The Woodlands, so she was going to be perfectly all right at Little Oreford Court, at least for the time being.
While Corrine was studying the aircraft' plasticated safety instructions sheet, dear Richard popped into her mind and how, so stupidly on the rebound from

Jonathan, she'd jetted off from here to spend a week with him at his home on Madeira.
He was a really nice, but lonely man, and she wondered whether he'd actually found a wife because he would make someone very happy. She reached out and squeezed Michael's hand, as if to purge herself of disloyal thoughts. He turned and gave her a smile.
She was sitting by the window with Michael next to her, and they were both anxiously watching the last few passengers making their way hesitantly down the aisle and peering up at seat numbers. It was a kind of Russian roulette, hoping that no one would take the seat next to them, thought Michael, who'd played the game many times around the world on fights out to catch up with his ship after a spot of shore leave, back in his executive chef days, but they were out of luck. 'Oh no,' he thought as a large lady, carrying what was clearly an oversized cabin bag, heaved her way towards them and shuddered to a stop beside him. "I think this must be mine," she puffed, looking up at the open locker. It was instantly clear that she'd never be able to lift her bulging bag up into the tiny space, already almost full of luggage. "Allow me to help," said Michael, squeezing past her to get out of his seat. "Thank you. That would be most kind, but I do need to get a few things out first,"

she said, hauling the bag up onto her empty seat and unzipping it to reveal a mad jumble of items, clearly all stuffed in at the last minute, and delving into it.
"I know my ear plugs are in here somewhere," she said, half to herself and half to Michael, as he stood helplessly looking at her.
All the other passenger were now seated and a stewardess was hurrying down the aisle towards them, closing all the still open overhead lockers as she passed, before coming to a stop beside Michael. "Don't worry madam we have complimentary ear plugs we can give you," she said as, sizing up the situation and taking command, she deftly zipped up the woman's bag, which Michael then stuffed into the overhead locker.
It was four long hours to the Canary Islands and both Michael and Corinne viewed the prospect with dismay, now effectively hemmed into their seats by, Hattie Holland, as she'd quickly introduced herself. It was a distinctive name that half rang a bell with both of them. Hattie kept up an almost continuous, but surprisingly humorous commentary, and worst of all, they discovered she was staying at their four-star hotel overlooking the Atlantic at Jandia Playa in the far south of the island.
"Thank God we have a private transfer," said Michael after, with quite a struggle, she'd got out of her seat and

gone to the toilet midway through the flight. "I actually think I quite like her," admitted Corinne, keeping her voice down. "She might be a bit overweight, but she's quick-witted and intelligent and it sounds like she's certainly had a most interesting life, travelling all over the world and, for some reason, her name sounds familiar," Corinne remarked quietly. "Funnily enough, I thought so too," whispered Michael, as he spotted her returning to her seat.

It was not long after Hattie had settled herself and had started talking about her recent amazing cruise to Antarctica, that the proverbial penny finally dropped. Quite by chance, Michael had scanned a full-page article about the icy continent in one of the Sunday papers, which a guest had obligingly left in the bar at The Cheringford. So that was it. Hattie Holland was the national travel writer, whose zany take on the world had a huge following wherever she went, and now she was off to cast her roving eye and her off-the-wall perspective over Fuerteventura.

Corinne and Michael said little as they sat back and relaxed in the semi-darkness of the limo, carrying them towards a stunning pink sunset with the black silhouettes of jagged peaks all around.

An hour later, they were gazing out from their balcony overlooking the silent Atlantic. Below, and standing out from the silky warm darkness, was an illuminated scene of palm trees and swimming pools, where chilling out was to be the priority for the following day. But, right now, it was time for supper in the hotel's exclusive bistro, reserved only for the handful of highest paying guests.
"I'm surprised Hattie's not here," remarked Corinne, casting her eye around at the few other obviously well-heeled diners, but hardly were the words out of her mouth, when there was a commotion at the bistro's entrance. "That's Hattie, so this is going to be interesting," replied Michael, noticing that most of the other diners were now looking up to see what all the fuss was about. But surprisingly little happened because, after being led to a booth at the back of the bistro by a white gloved waiter carrying what was clearly a laptop case, their fellow traveller settled down with a large glass of red wine and was not heard from again.
"I do so love you Michael, but I think I'm really too tired for playing tonight," she whispered, after he'd climbed into the enormous bed and was snuggling up beside her and sliding a gently probing hand up under her night shirt. 'We both always seem to be too tired these days,' he thought as he reluctantly withdrew, but no doubt,

they'd both feel far more relaxed after a few days in the sun.
They got up around nine and taking the lift down to the upper pool level, exclusively reserved for the comparatively few gold-star guests, walked around the water's edge, lined with still empty sunbeds, to an open windowed restaurant looking straight out over the ocean.
"This is bliss," said Corinne, after they'd taken a table on the exterior decking area in the already surprisingly warm sunshine. They'd just been inside and helped themselves to starters from the most exotic display of fresh fruits, and a whole array of other dishes, that even Michael had to admit, was outstanding.
They spent the next two days swimming, reading books and chilling out around the quiet pool area until around four. Then, after being served tea and cakes by a pretty, young waitress carrying a silver tray, they'd headed out for a walk along the long sandy beach towards the small resort of Morro Jable.
"I think I've rested enough, so tomorrow let's hire a car and a driver to take us off on a tour of the island," suggested Michael. as they strolled back to the hotel to dress for dinner.
"Great idea," replied Corinne. She'd discovered that, while lazing around and relaxing by the pool and re

charging her batteries had been just what she needed, she was a doing person, and that, actually, one day would have been enough, but it was to be a fateful decision!

Chapter 12

George Simpkins drove into Glastonbury on a wet, cold, and dreary Sunday afternoon and was surprised just how busy the High Street was. This was in sharp contrast to most of the other towns and villages he'd driven through, having decided to come off the M4 at Bath and make his way across country.

All the shops were open and the pavements were crowded as he drove slowly along looking for a place to park, which seemed like it was not going to happen until a delivery van obligingly pulled out just ahead of him. Leaving his small overnight bag in the car, he went in search of his hotel, which he knew from the directions he'd been given, had to be close by.

As he'd volunteered his services on a no win no fee basis, and the Jameson family were paying his expenses, then a comfortable hotel with a restaurant and bar where he could enjoy a before and after pint in the bar, was definitely his preferred option. This was certainly a wacky town he decided, glancing sideways into the shops displaying candles and a whole host of alternative wares, and catching the distinct aroma of incense and slowly burning joss sticks on the crowded air.

He'd glimpsed Glastonbury's famous tor, rising sharply, one hundred and fifty-eight metres above the surrounding countryside on his way into town and had also passed the, almost as famous, ruined abbey. But all this historical and alternative stuff was definitely not his bag. When it came to finding out what had become of Rachael Jefferson and her daughter Anna, there was certainly not much to go on George mused.

Enjoying a quiet pre-dinner drink in the centuries old hotel's oak beamed bar, he peered down at the yellowing sheet of notepaper with the heading New Grimsby House, Glastonbury, 1984. He'd overcome the Jamesons' initial reluctance to letting him borrow it, and it was now lying on the bar table in front of him. Yes, all the clues were in the note, he thought, studying the script, clearly written by a neat hand. Of course, all he really needed from it, was the information that they were now living at New Grimsby House and that Anna had settled in well at the local junior school. But somehow having the woman's actual letter in his possession, was comforting. It was somehow like a small, but solid rock in a sea of uncertainty. New Grimsby House sounded rather grand and where indeed was it to be found in this interesting town? he mused. And then again, where was New Grimsby itself and might even this name have

some remote bearing on the case before him? When one had so few clues, even the smallest thread of a lead could not be discounted.
New Grimsby sounded like it might be somewhere in the New World, possibly Tasmania, because all those early seafaring adventurers certainly had a habit of naming new places after familiar ones to remind them of home. He'd thought of Tasmania because he'd been there in his younger days, and had been particularly struck by just how many places had been named after the old country, including a busy town call Launceston, with its own River Tamar.
George picked up the phone, from where it lay on the table beside him with a copy of the local paper, and Googled New Grimsby. Now there was a surprise.
It wasn't in the New World, but much closer to home as a small harbourside community on the almost sub-tropical island of Tresco, some twenty-eight miles beyond Land's End in the Isles of Scilly.
Thankfully, the weather had cleared overnight, and George was greeted by a blue sky, on stepping outside, around nine, on a crisp, cold, Monday morning to go in search of a postie on his rounds. For if anyone around here was going to know where New Grimsby House was to be found, then it was the postie. They were nearly

always a mine of information, especially the older ones, who'd often trudged the same familiar streets for years. It was on many a previous occasion, going back to his early days on a copper's beat, that a postie had been able to point him in the right direction when it came to finding an address. This particular morning, George was out of luck, because it was almost an hour before he spotted a familiar red van. But even that had its advantages, because he'd certainly needed the exercise, after spending hours in the car the previous day. Now he had the town's geography pretty much mapped out, including the whereabouts of the local primary school, which would be his next port of call. Yes, this postwoman certainly knew where New Grimsby House was to be found and that was luckily, only a couple of roads away. In George's mind's eye, this was a substantial Victorian or Edwardian property, set in a large garden, but, no, it was in the middle of a neat row of, Victorian villas with limestone garden walls and fancy wrought-iron gates.

A few steps brought him to the front door where he softly wrapped on the ornate metal knocker and waited, but no one was at home.

"That's a pain," he muttered, turning and heading for the school.' But no, change of plan, he thought, spotting the

entrance to a small well-kept park and an inviting seat now in full sun.
George fished out his notebook and phone and looked up the number of the local newspaper, he'd jotted down, while browsing though it over his pint the previous evening, and asked to speak with someone in the newsroom. A woman answered and he was instantly attracted by the melodic sound of her voice. George introduced himself, explaining that he had a small news story, if there was someone there who might help him. "I certainly can. So, what's it about?" she asked. "I would like to appeal to your older readers for any information they might have, concerning a woman called, Rachael Jefferson, and her daughter, Anna.
They lived in Glastonbury in the mid 1970s, where the girl was a pupil at the local school," he explained. "That sounds most intriguing, so why are you looking for them?" might ask, Mr Simpkins?" George told her he was making a few enquiries on behalf of a family, who had lost touch with her and wanted to discuss an inheritance, "So, are you a private investigator and is it a very large inheritance?" she asked. "I guess I am something like that, but I'm not at liberty to disclose the sum involved," George told her. "How exciting," said the woman, introducing herself as Sandy Loxton. She was

the paper's Features Editor, and was now beginning to fish for a story, because she'd never written about a private detective before, and now she had one nibbling on the end of her telephone line. "I can probably squeeze a small appeal into this week's paper. But if we left it until next week, I could write a piece about you and your work and make it a much bigger and eye-catching story," she offered.

"That's extremely kind of you Sandy, but I'm only here for a couple of days and don't have the time to stay around for a week," he explained. "OK, I'll see what I can do, but if you should change your mind about the story, I would really enjoy writing it."

For a moment George faltered. He liked the sound of her voice and it might be nice spending an evening with her, and who knows where that might lead? But no, he was by nature a private person, which was something of an irony, seeing that he liked to be the one asking all the questions and certainly not answering them. He thanked her again for her offer and after leaving her his phone number, started walking slowly and thoughtfully in the direction of the school. Getting access to schools was such a pain these days, because of all the security measures, compared with earlier and more innocent times, when one could just walk in, he thought, as he stood outside the gate tapping the telephone number on the noticeboard into his mobile. The phone only rang a couple of times before the message recording kicked in and he pressed option four for the Secretaries' Office. George briefly explained the reason for his enquiry, wondering if there might be any retired teachers living in the area who taught at the school in the mid1970s. He was half expecting to be quickly fobbed off with the data protection line that they could not possibly give out any details concerning retired staff. But not for the first time on that sunny morning, George was in luck, because the secretary had gone to the loo and the phone had been picked up by the headmistress, who was now nearing retirement herself and for whom the name Anna Jefferson did ring a bell.

Five minutes later, he was sitting in front of Miss Florence Carson's desk, with its piled high in-tray, and had a welcome mug of coffee in his hand. "You would not want to be running a school these days, Mr Simpkins, because I seem to spend all my time complying with a constant stream of new directives, issued from on high," she said, spotting him glancing at her unremitting pile of paperwork. It was as if the floodgates had opened and she felt completely safe unburdening herself to this well-dressed and kindly looking stranger. "When I started at this school, I'd take my class out on Wednesday afternoon nature rambles, but we can't even move these days without filling in long-winded risk assessment forms." She paused, as if suddenly remembering the reason for her visitor's enquiry. That was it. That was why the name, Anna Jefferson, rang a bell because the child had been so passionate about nature. "Yes, Mr Simpkins, I do remember Anna because she was the one girl who shone on our nature walks," she told him. "How do you mean shone?" asked George, who had earlier explained about the bequeath being the reason he was trying to find the Jeffersons. "For one thing, I think she must have had a photographic memory, because she always remembered the names of all the plants and trees we identified. But, more than that, when the class returned with leaves to paint, her paintings and drawings were always by far the best and I could see she had the makings of a very talented artist. It's funny, Mr Simpkins, because you don't have to be teaching long before you can identify the youngsters with that little extra something, which may mean they will most probably get on well in life and Anna Jefferson certainly had that little extra something," she explained.

“Do you happen to remember her mother?” George asked tentatively. “Yes, I do because I met her several times when she came along to parents’ evenings, usually with an older man, whom I seem to recall was her uncle, but of course, I can’t be sure. Mrs Jefferson was an attractive and well-dressed woman, but seemed to me to be quite highly strung, if you know what I mean,” she added. “I don’t suppose you can remember what happened to them?” George asked. The headmistress shook her head. “Literally hundreds of families come into one’s orbit and then out again over the years and, while one does tend to keep track on the local families, especially when they suddenly reappear as parents with children of their own. But I’m afraid the Jeffersons did not fall into that category,” she said. George thanked her for sparing him so much of her valuable time and gave her his card, asking her to get back in touch if, by any chance, she might later remember anything else which she thought might be of assistance.

In the perfect world of his enquiries, young Anna Jefferson would have gone on to meet and marry a local lad and would have been a parent at that school, he mused, as he made his way slowly back towards New Grimsby House. But this was not a perfect world, which it had been when he so easily fulfilled his last assignment by discovering the whereabouts of one Chrissy Morales.

Chapter 13

Completely refreshed after two days of rest and relaxation, Corinne and Michael were standing outside the hotel foyer in the already warm morning sunshine, waiting for their previously booked car and driver to show up, when they suddenly heard a familiar voice behind them "Hi! where have you two been hiding away for the past couple of days? Are you waiting for a taxi into the town because, if so, then perhaps we might share the cost?" suggested a familiar voice. "Oh! hi Hattie. No, we have a guide with a car booked for a whole day island tour," replied Corinne. The words just slipped out because after being so rested she had been caught completely off her guard. "Oh, do you?"

"So, if it's not a terribly small car, perhaps I could join you and share the cost and treat you both to lunch," Hattie suggested. They were well and truly cornered because to say no would sound so churlish. But Michael was made of sterner stuff. The prospect of spending a whole precious day being couped up in a small car with Hattie Holland keeping up an inane commentary was definitely more than he could tolerate. But before he could think up a diplomatic way of declining her kind invitation, their transport arrived. It wasn't a small car, which under normal circumstances would have disappointed them, but a large air-conditioned people carrier and before he could say another word, the young driver, who'd introduced himself as Franco, had leapt out and slid open its copious door. It was a fete accompli and he knew it. "Go on then," he said smiling weakly at Hattie, who needing no further bidding, climbed into the back seat with a remarkable agility.

So, she can move when she wants to, Michael thought, as he and Corinne exchanged glances and took the four middle seats, one at each window, and belted up. They drove for some twenty minutes back along the coast road, before turning off the highway and beginning to climb inland. Their eventual lunchtime destination was Betancuria, the island's former green oasis of a capital, founded high in the central hills, and relatively safe from the Barbary pirates, Franco explained. He'd kept up an easy commentary, punctuated by quite long silences, which they'd initially feared Hattie would fill the void, but no, she sat quietly, just asking the occasional intelligent question, that actually contributed to the experience, so perhaps the day was going to turn out OK after all, thought Corinne.

Their first stop was a magnificent viewpoint, overlooking a wide and biblical landscape, which had actually been used in the making of films, including Exodus and Star Wars, Franco explained as he stood beside them. Turning, he showed them an impressive stone gateway, seemingly in the middle of nowhere, which actually marked the entrance and exit to one of the island's six municipalities, he told he told them. "But why is there a sign asking people not to feed the squirrels when there isn't a tree for miles around?" asked Hattie. With that, one of the creatures obligingly hopped onto a nearby wall and seemed to wink knowingly at them. They all reached for their mobiles to grab a picture of him, but when they looked again, he had gone. These were Barbary Squirrels, introduced by accident from North Africa in the 1960s, and because they had no predators, there were now millions of them all over the island, Franco explained.

"They look like cute Chipmunks, but they eat almost anything, including all the succulents and small plants that struggled to grow in our arid environment, so they are a real pest," he said, turning to lead the way back to their vehicle.

"Our next stop is to be the village of Vega del Rio Palmas, the scene of a pilgrimage to the shrine of the island's patron saint, every September," he told them, after they had been driving for a few minutes. "It has a pleasant square and is worth having a stroll around, with somewhere to stop for a coffee if you like."

It was the last sentence poor Franco was ever to utter. The next moment, a frantic truck driver, whose brakes had failed further up the hill, and had lost control on a small bend, came crashing into them. Franco took the full impact of the blow, which pushed them off the road and sent them rolling down the sloping hillside with Michael, who was sitting on the driver's side, taking the full impact of the first roll. It was all over in a few wild and metal tearing, upside down seconds, when, mercifully, the people carrier smashed into a large rock and came to a dead stop on its side. Corinne, now hanging in her seatbelt, sideways over Michael, was the first to recover her senses. She saw that he was not moving and appeared to be unconscious. "Where am I?" "What happened?" she heard Hattie's confused and mumbling voice behind her. There was no sound from Franco, whose bent left arm was all she could see between the seats. Then her vision began blurring at the edges and she lapsed into unconsciousness. When she came around, she was lying on a stretcher with Hattie peering anxiously down at her. "Oh, thank God your back," she said. "Where's Michael. Is he all right too?" she whispered.

Now a paramedic was leaning over her while talking rapidly to Hattie in Spanish. "He says Michael has head injuries and is being taken to the island's main hospital in Puerto del Rosario." Hattie explained. "Oh! poor Michael. I must go with him," Corinne cried out, as she attempted to get up, but felt the gently restraining hand of the paramedic holding her back, as he was again speaking to Hattie. "He says you must lie still while he examines you to make sure nothing is broken." Corinne obeyed. "But what about Franco?" she asked. "I'm afraid he's beyond help," said Hattie quietly. "Oh no," said Corinne, her eyes beginning to fill with tears, as the paramedic continued conversing with Hattie in rapid Spanish. "He says he wants you to try moving your limbs very slowly and one at a time," Hattie explained. A few minutes later, Corinne was being helped to her feet and she and Hattie were being escorted slowly back up the hillside, past the dented remains of their vehicle. It was still surrounded by firefighters, one of whom came over with Corinne's shoulder bag, its leather strap torn off at one end, and Hattie's battered, but unopened holdall, and began talking to them earnestly. "Tell him I must go with Michael," pleaded Corinne, but she could see that this man, who appeared to be in charge, was shaking his head. "He says that isn't possible and that we'll be taken

back to our hotel to rest and can visit Michael later, explained Hattie. "I still can't believe this is happening," whispered Corinne, tears pouring down her face, as the paramedic support vehicle began nosing its way slowly back down the hill.
They passed the lorry that had ended up just off the road, but still upright and a huge tailback of mostly holiday traffic. "Michael is going to be all right, isn't he?" asked Corinne, desperate for a comforting answer. "I'm sure he will and we'll call the hospital in a couple of hours, by which time they will have been able to assess his injuries, Hattie reassured her. "Oh Hattie, thank goodness you speak Spanish and that you came with us," said Corinne, instinctively giving her arm a gentle squeeze. Back at the hotel, Corinne, whose back had now started aching and left elbow was painfully sore, took the lift up to their suit, accompanied by a woman member of the hotel team. Still feeling slightly dazed and completely unreal, and leaving a trail of dirt-stained clothes behind her, she made her way slowly into the shower and allowed the warm water to caress her aching body. "Michael, my poor Michael," she cried as her tears were washed away.

Chapter 14

Dr Albert Flavell could hear the persistent ringing of the phone in his study. At first, he took no notice because, after all, it was eight am on a Sunday morning, but after a couple of minutes he could ignore it no longer. “Dad why was your mobile switched off? I’ve been trying to call you for ages.” Roxanne sounded far more upset than accusatory and Albert picked up on that immediately “What on earth’s the matter?” There was a pause. “Luke and I have decided to split up and go our separate ways for a while.” Dr Flavell took a few moments to take in the shock announcement. “What! I know you’ve been having a few ups and downs lately, but I never dreamed it would come to this. Have you thought of the terrible effect this is going to have on Luca?

“Surely you can’t be serious. You’ve just had a bad row and you can’t possibly be thinking straight,” he told her. “No Dad, we are serious this time,” she replied. “What do you mean, serious this time? Are you telling me there have been other times when you’ve both come to this conclusion?” he demanded. Dad it’s no good. He could hear she was getting heated. “We’ve simply fallen out of love and we can’t go on like this. Albert knew his

daughter was strong willed like her mother. "Have you both thought seriously about what this will do my poor little grandson? He's only five for heaven's sake," Albert persisted.
"Dad it's far better that we have some time apart to give us some space to think things through," she replied.
"That's just the stock answer and I won't go along with it until I'm clear in my own mind that this is really what you both want," he told her.
"Please bear with me over this, at least for a couple more months. Now can I speak to Luke to hear what he has to say?" he asked. "No, you can't Dad, because he's taken Luca out to get the Sunday papers. But he'll call you when he gets back, but we have both really made up our minds over this," she persisted. 'Bloody kids. They had no staying power these days. Roxanne was used to having her own way. He had over indulged her and he knew it and this was the result,' he chided himself.
Luke was strolling back across the park, feeling a mixture of relief and sadness, while Luca trotting happily along beside him. Sadness that what had started out with so much promise with their passion to help save the world from climate change, had managed to turn so sour. Luca had been an accident and a reality check.

Now they had real responsibilities and could no longer throw in their lectureships on a whim and jet off to who knows where. To make things a whole lot worse, he'd quickly discovered that Roxanne did not appear to have a single maternal instinct in her entire being. So, he was the one who did most of the caring for their son and was the one the little fellow instinctively felt closest to, apart for his doting grandpapa, that was. They'd agreed he should take the child home to Little Oreford, where he knew his whole extended family would be there to support them both until they could work out a new direction, and that was a relief. But he knew in his heart of hearts that they'd never get back together again. 'I've really made a mess of my life,' he chided himself, now thinking of his previous partner, who had so wanted to settle down and have a family.

He had been very close to her for a long time and wondered where she was and what she might be doing now. It was Uncle Robin's out of the blue £250,000 legacy that had finally put paid to his marriage. He'd wanted to use the cash to pay off the last of the mortgage they had left over, after they'd swapped Roxanne's loft conversion, funded by her father, for a more suitable semi-detached family home. But she'd wanted them to donate a large portion of it to her latest climate change project. "We should be putting some of that money where our mouths are, can't you see that?" she'd told him on their drive back to London after the funeral. But Luke did not see. It was all very well for her to take such an altruistic view. Her globe-trotting activism had been entirely funded by her father, on whose cash support she could always depend, and could go on depending until she inevitable inherited his wealth. But for him it was different because, having got by on very little all his life, this cash represented a solid investment that should not simply be frittered away on some whim, especially as they now had Luca to think about. OK he knew that as long as he and Roxanne were together, he too could count on Dr Albert Flavell's generous support, but the idea of being so ultimately dependent on him somehow made him feel inadequate. The income from their lectureships just about covered their mortgage and their living expenses, so inevitably when they needed anything, like the expensive trampoline for Luca, it was Albert who'd happily paid for it. While the legacy had been the flash point for their latest and most serious row, it would at least buy him a lot of breathing space when he and Luca got home to Little Oreford.

"Dad says we should wait at least a couple of months before splitting, but I don't really see the point, do you?"

Roxanne challenged almost as soon as he got through the door and Luca was up in his bedroom playing happily by himself. “No, I don’t either,” Luke agreed. The truth was that his wife had become almost unbearable with her totally unrealistic schemes for taking off around the world with their child in tow, while he had settled well into his lectureship and was enjoying working with his students. “It’s far more important to use our time and energies, inspiring the younger generation to get involved with our mission, rather than go on doing stuff ourselves. Can’t you see that for heaven’s sake?” he’d argued on numerous occasions.

But Roxanne, whose wanderlust had, in reality, become a sickness, could not see that and he knew she never would. The thing was that while he had settled down and was enjoying his job, she was definitely not and had come home frustrated and unhappy most evenings, which had inevitably led to all manner of tensions. Her latest wildcat scheme had been to use his legacy to fund their taking off with Luca and joining a save the rainforest project in the Amazon basin. When Luke had told her, in the heat of the moment, there was no way he was ever going to do that, and if she felt that strongly about it, then she should go off and do it by herself, she had replied that if that was how he really felt then, that's just what she'd do.

Chapter 15

Laura and Ben were just finishing a quiet lunch together when the phone rang and she got up from the kitchen table to answer it. "Oh Laura, Michael and I have been involved in a terrible accident." She could tell instantly that her twin sister was dreadfully upset. "Where are you both and what happened?" Laura asked, switching the phone to speaker mode. "We're in the island's hospital where Michael was brought after our car was his hit by a truck," she replied flatly. "Corinne that's terrible. What happened? She questioned. "He was knocked unconscious, but still hasn't come around yet, although it was hours ago. Hattie, a friend we'd made on holiday, and I were just badly bruised and shaken, but our poor driver guide was killed." Laura could hear her sister beginning to cry. "Oh no, that's awful, you poor girl. So what's happening now?" she questioned. "Hattie and I got here about an hour ago. She insisted on coming with me because, thankfully, she speaks Spanish. To start with we were in this large hospital waiting area with a lot of other people, but now we're sitting in a corridor waiting for someone to see us. I think this might be her coming now, so I'll call you back". The line went dead. "Oh God. I can't believe it. They so needed that break and now this has happened and what if he lapses into a coma?" asked Laura, turning to Ben. "Look he'll probably come around in a couple of hours," he reassured her. "Don't forget, I had a lot of experience of head injury situations when I was the administrator at the County General, so we must just wait and see." Laura sat down at the kitchen table.

"Oh! Ben, I do hope you're right. Five minutes later and just after Ben had left to go back to The Old Mill House for the afternoon, the phone rang again and Laura grabbed it. "Mum it's me," said Luke. "Are you all right because you sounded a bit weird when you answered the phone?" he asked. "Yes dear. I am all right, but I'm feeling really worried because Auntie Corinne and Michael have just been involved in a horrible accident, while on holiday in the Canary Islands," she replied, hurriedly explaining what had happened. "That's terrible," said Luke, now doing some rapid rethinking as he wandered around an empty college classroom on his mobile phone. He had planned to break the news about him and Roxanne before inviting himself and Luca down for a long weekend, but this was now clearly not the time for explanations. "Mum, Roxanne is busy on a project this weekend, so I was wondering if me and Luca could come down for a couple of days, but maybe this might not be the time seeing what's happened," he suggested. "No, do come because dad thinks that Michael will probably be OK and it would be lovely to see you."

George Simpkins, thanked the Junior School headmistress for the coffee and stepped back out into the late morning sunshine. He retraced his steps to New Grimsby House, but there was still no one at home, which meant the occupants were probably at work and he'd have to return in the early evening. 'Time for some lunch, I think, and then maybe take a stroll around the abbey grounds, but I'll give climbing the tor a miss because, although it's sunny, it's still bloody cold,' he told himself.
It was just after seven when he again called at New Grimsby House. The door was opened by a woman, probably in her early fifties. She had a rounded, open and friendly face and gave him an enquiring look. George knew a benign expression when he encountered one, having been met with so many uncertain and challenging ones during the countless days he'd spent knocking on doors, both while with the police and on his own account. "Would you like to come in?" she invited, after he'd quickly explained the reason for his call. George followed her into what would have been the old

front room, before it was knocked through into the kitchen, to form a large open plan space, and was introduced to the woman's husband, who said his mission all sounded rather intriguing. They were Andrew and Sally Monkton and explained they'd bought the house in the late 1990s and that 'yes,' they did remember a little about the previous owner. It was more sweet music to George's ears.

"He was pretty elderly and lived on his own and the place had been totally neglected for years. We had to spend a month clearing out all his junk and making the place habitable again before we could move in, didn't we Andy?" she said. "I don't suppose you remember his name, do you?" George asked tentatively. "Well yes, actually I do, because it was Lionel Horsefall and my sister happened to take a fall from her horse at around the same time," recalled Sally. "And there's something more we can tell you because he was quite a celebrated historian and we donated loads of his books and papers to the local history society," recalled Andy. 'Now I have another lead," George told himself, after he'd thanked the couple for their help and was making his way back to the hotel for a pre-dinner pint. There was steak and kidney pudding with a rich gravy on the menu and he was definitely a steak and kidney pudding man. It was

far too late to call The Journal now, but he would do so first thing in the morning.
"May I speak with Sally Loxton please," he asked the paper's receptionist, She put him straight through. "Sally, it's George Simpkins with another favour to ask." He'd got good vibes from their last, albeit quite brief conversation, and decided she was a woman with whom he could risk a little informality and he was right. "What! not you again, and on deadline day when I'm really busy," she bantered. "OK I'll be brief because I only want to know if you can give me a contact for the local history society, if it's still in being, that is?" he added. "All these demands. I don't know, but give me a moment. There was a 'click' and the line appeared to go dead. George hung on. He was sitting on the side of his hotel bed, after breakfast, and vaguely beginning to wonder if he might entice this most obliging woman into it after a nice intimate supper in the hotel restaurant. 'Dream on sunshine,' he told himself. It was one of his favourite reality checks, but just as he was beginning to think he'd been cut off, she was back. "Try Charles Hooper. He was the chairman the last time I spoke to them, so here's his number. Do let me know how you get on, but now I really must go," she said putting the phone down

on him. George was delighted. Here was another lead and it came with an open invitation to call Sally back.
"Yes, I certainly remember Lionel," said the history society chairman, who was in the middle of his breakfast when George called.
"He was the chairman when I joined on moving to Glastonbury, but he sadly died not long afterwards, so, I don't really know much about him. But Cyril North, our oldest member, surely will because I think they were quite close," he explained. "And where might I find him?" enquired George. "That's easy. He is well into his nineties and lives at Sunny Bank. It's a row of bungalows quite close to the abbey, although not that easy to find. But I suppose I could take you there and introduce you, if you like, because I've not got much else going on this morning." George said that would be most helpful and they arranged to meet outside the abbey in an hour.
Widowed, and now early retired estate agent, Charles Hooper, gave George a potted version of his entire life story on the twenty minute walk to Sunny Bank. He warned him that Cyril was an amazing ninety-four-year-old who could talk the hind legs of the proverbial donkey, which amused George, especially coming from him.
"Another amazing thing about Cyril is that he's totally embraced the world of the Internet and is busy putting all

our records, going back hundreds of years, on line for the whole world to read," he revealed. "That is amazing," George agreed. "I gave Cyril a call, so he's expecting us," said Charles as they approached his front door. "How interesting, Mr Simpkins, and, yes, I will do all I can to help you with the aid of my wonderful friend the Internet, which gives us access to our whole fascinating world at our fingertips," said Cyril, who was small, neat and bursting with energy. "If I'd been told when I was growing up that, one day, I'd be able to see and talk to someone on the other side of the world, via a tiny screen, held in the palm of my hand, I would have thought them crazy.
Now what would you like me to tell you about dear Lionel, because we were very close for a lot of years you know?" he revealed. "It's not actually him I am interested in, but a woman called, Rachael Jefferson, and her daughter, Anna, who I think came to live with him, probably in the early 1970s. I believe they may have been relations and stayed with him for at least a couple of years, because the daughter went to the local junior school," George explained. "Yes, of course I remember them. How could I not because she was a most attractive woman and the daughter was extremely bright you know. Rachael was his niece. She just turned up on

his doorstep one day and gave poor Lionel the fright of his life, but he took them in and they did live with him for several years. He was a confirmed bachelor and very stuck in his ways and there was a lot of friction," he recalled. "So, what happened them, Cyril?" George asked, knowing he'd finally arrived at another key fork along the road of his so far most successful enquiries. "Rachael was Lionel's younger sister Ivy Jefferson's child. The family came from Richmond and were quite wealthy, but retired to St Ives after Rachael had left home. She was their only child and had been spoilt rotten by them, but she was wayward and had a big falling out with them, which was why she'd turned up on poor Lionel's doorstep. George could not believe his continuing good luck. "How do you remember all this Cyril?" he asked. "That was because Lionel would tell me his continuing tale of woe over a couple of pints at our local. Eventually, he managed to broker a truce between his sister and his niece and she and Anna moved to St Ives and that is the end of the story, as far as I know, because Lionel made a point of steering well clear of his sister and his niece after that," he explained. "I can't tell you just how helpful you've been Cyril," George said, as he got up to leave. Thirty minutes later, he'd checked out of the hotel and was on his way to

Cornwall. ‘It would have been nice to have delayed and possibly taken that most helpful journalist Sally Loxton out to supper,’ he mused, as the famous Glastonbury Tor slipped below the horizon.

Chapter 16

The concerned look on the Spanish doctor's face as he came towards them was not reassuring, but thankfully, Antonio Garcia, as his name badge told them, spoke English extremely well and led the way back along the corridor and into a small office, where he invited them to take a seat. "I'm afraid your husband has received a severe blow to the head and has not recovered consciousness, but we will have a better understanding of the seriousness of his condition after we have the results of some MRI scans, which he will be doing very shortly," he explained. "When can I see my husband?" she questioned. "We are extremely busy with emergencies at the moment and, as I said, we are about to start the scanning procedure, so hopefully later on this afternoon, but now if you will excuse me, I do have to go."

Corinne and Hattie made their way back through the hospital's maze of corridors to the large waiting room, which seemed even busier than when they'd arrived. "Let's go and find a coffee somewhere outside in the sunshine," suggested Hattie. They found a vendor and a bench in partial shade and Corinne phoned Laura, trying to keep back her tears as she updated her. "Do try not to worry because I'm sure it's all going to be all right," her sister reassured her, before ringing off. "Look Hattie. This is your holiday and there's no need for you to stay with me if you don't want to," Corinne suggested, after a few moments silence. "No, we're in this together and while that doctor spoke English, you may see someone else who doesn't when we go back in," she pointed out. "Well, if you're sure because it may be a long to wait." They went back into the hospital at three and queued to see a receptionist, who after making several phone calls in rapid Spanish, suggested to Hattie they come back around six. "The longer this goes on, the more I think Michael's situation must be extremely serious," said Corinne as they made their way back to the seat only to find it occupied. "Perhaps we should head out and find a small café, or a bar, because I'm feeling in need of some sustenance," said Hattie. "I don't feel I could eat a thing, but you must be starving," said Corinne apologizing. They returned to the hospital at six, but it was just after seven when a nurse came to collect them and took them back up to the same little office where Doctor Garcia was waiting. Corinne could see instantly that his face was full of concern. "I'm afraid that your husband is still consciousness and its now going to be a case of close monitoring until he comes around," he explained. "He is going to come around isn't he doctor?" She asked. "He has lapsed into a coma that may last a few hours, or could go on for several weeks, or even up to a month, but very rarely beyond that," he assured her. "And he is going to be OK when he comes around, isn't he?" Corinne pressed. It was a question, Antonio Garcia, had faced from mostly distraught tourists, on a number of occasions since he'd embarked on his career in complex neurosurgery. "All I can tell you is that in Michael's case, it does look as if he may well make a full recovery, but it really is impossible to say until he regains consciousness. So perhaps you would like to see him now," he said, talking in Spanish to a nurse, standing in the doorway behind them.

They found Michael in a small private room all wired up, as in the hospital dramas, and with a large bandage around his head. "Oh! my poor darling," said Corinne, taking the empty chair beside the bed. Hattie hung back and then decided it was best not to come in. Michael was lying on his back with his arms resting outside the sheet. She leaned forward and took his hand. It was soft and warm to the touch and somehow, that one small physical contact, reassured her that he was going to come back to her "Oh! my poor Michael, do you remember how we first met? Well, of course you do," she said answering her own question. "It was when came to see you at your catering college to tell you that The Oreford would be delighted to offer your trainee chefs some work experience. Corinne went on recalling her early memories of their budding relationship until, ten minutes later, a nurse came in and told her it was time to leave.

They found several taxies outside and climbed into the smartest one. It set off at high speed until, speaking in rapid Spanish, Hattie explained what had happened to them. The driver slowed down immediately and, overcome by physical and mental exhaustion, they dozed for most of the ride back to the hotel.

When they pulled up on the brightly lit forecourt, Hattie insisted on paying and in a conversation that went on for several minutes, the driver, who was called Marco, said he was sorry to hear how their holiday on his beautiful island had been ruined. He was new to being a taxi driver and had a young family to support so he would give them a special rate for all their journeys to and from the hospital if they called him.

"Would you like to go to the bar for a drink and a snack, or shall we meet for breakfast in the morning before we go back to the hospital," Hattie, asked. "Look Hattie, I'm extremely grateful for all your help today, but do you really don't need to come back with me again tomorrow and ruin any more of your precious days?" she asked. "Yes, I do because we are in this together and, who knows, what practical assistance you are going to need in the days to come. I am a completely free agent and I won't be flying home while you still need my help," she declared. "Oh Hattie. That's so kind of you and maybe now I do feel in need of a drink after all we've been through today," she conceded. "That's good and I really do think you should have something to eat to keep your strength up for Michael's sake."

Chapter 17

"We've been invited over to Alicia and Shaun's for lunch tomorrow," announced Annie, as Bob and Olivia came in after playing in the garden. "That's great because we haven't seen them for a while," he said. "Yes, but I don't want you disappearing off with Anthony to play with the cars at your first opportunity," Annie replied, but it was half in jest. "Just as if I would do that," he responded, although he knew she was joking. "Alicia says we might like to come, say around 11am, and bring our swimming things, so that Olivia and Corina can have a splash around in the pool before lunch," she explained. "All sounds good to me, but talking of lunch, what shall we have today?" he asked. Annie would normally have been behind reception at The Oreford on a Monday. But the inn was still closed and would not be reopening until Corinne and Michael got back from the Canary Islands, so the family were enjoying a most welcome quiet period in their busy lives.

"Just make yourselves at home as usual because Alicia and Corina are already in the pool, and you know where everything is," invited Shaun, as soon as he'd opened the door to them. "I think I'm going to give the pool a miss this morning," said Bob, who'd never been a lover of water, whether in it or sailing over it. “Great, then come and join me in the kitchen where I’ve been left in charge of lunch.”

It was around 3pm while they were sitting chatting over the remains of their meal at the kitchen table that Alicia finally raised the question that had now been on her mind for some weeks.

It was an opportune moment because Corina and Olivia had just gone off to play. “We’ve got something to ask you and it’s to do with our moving to Toronto in the summer, haven’t we Shaun?” said Alicia, suddenly reaching out and taking his hand in some instinctive act of solidarity. “We have absolutely no intention of letting go of The Woodlands. So, we’re wondering if you guys might just be prepared to move over here and look after the place for us,” she asked them. “Blimey!” said Bob looking at Annie. It was an old saying he’d picked up from his father. “Yes ‘blimey’ indeed,” replied Annie, struggling to rationalise the enormity of the ask. “When Alicia says ‘look after the place,’ she doesn’t mean that literally,” Shaun added. “We’ll still be keeping on Fred, our gardener, because he’s part of the furniture anyway, and Lizzy our cleaner, will still be over most days, if you were to be here. Also, the pool maintenance man will still be coming once a week. So, it just seems a shame to us if there's going to be nobody here to enjoy the place," he added. "And we wouldn't want you to pay any rent or anything like that," added Alicia. Annie and Bob looked at one another in disbelief. "That's an amazing offer, but what would happen when you come back for your summer holidays and we're living here?" asked Annie, feeling a stir of excitement at the prospect of having all this luxury so suddenly and unexpectedly, dropped into their laps. "That won't be a problem because this house is plenty big enough for two small families, who are really good friends anyway. But if you wanted to do a house swap and spend the summer exploring Toronto, then be our guests," invited Shaun.

Bob was already thinking of all the extra time he would have to spend with the car collection, but as ever, he was the more cautious one. "It is a most generous offer, but perhaps you could give us a few days to think about it," he said, although he already knew what their answer would most likely to be. "Look there's absolutely no rush to make up your minds because it's still months before we go, but there is one other option," said Alicia.

"We're certainly not going to be looking for anyone else to move in while we're in Toronto, so if you want to stay at Little Oreford Court, then perhaps, Bob, we could pay

you to pop over most days to keep an eye on the place and to play with the cars, of course," she joked.
Before he had time to respond, the phone on the kitchen wall sprang into life. Shaun got up to answer it and listened for a few moments. "It's Laura for you my love," he said, handing over the receiver. Alicia listened in a shocked silence, asking the occasional question, as Laura broke the news about the accident. The others quickly picked up that something terrible had happened. "I've also been trying to get hold of Annie and Bob, who mum says are having lunch with you," said Laura.
"That's right, they're here, so I'll pass you over to Annie.
When she'd finally put the phone down, they all sat, silently absorbing the awful news. "This could not have happened at a worse time," said Annie, now thinking of all that must lay ahead for her in her role as Acting Manager. "There's no way Corinne's going to be back at the weekend to open The Oreford on Monday and we already have guests booked in for later in the week. And then what are we going to do over at The Cheringford without Michael there?" she asked, as if still thinking aloud.
Bob agreed it was not going to be easy. "Annie, you, Laura and Ben are certainly going to have your hands full. But look, I'm sure there will be things I can also do to

help because Olivia will be back at school next week, as will the twins, so that will also free Lottie up to help," he pointed out. Alicia and Shaun suggested that perhaps it was time to bring their luncheon to a close in the circumstances, especially as Annie had now promised to go over and see Laura and Ben as soon as they got back.

Annie said little on the drive back to Little Oreford Court and Bob knew she would already have gone into work planning mode and that Alicia and Shaun's amazing offer was something they would talk about later. He wondered how Charlie would feel about it, especially as Lottie and Andy had already moved back into the village but he knew she'd never stand in their way

Chapter 18

Almost a week had now passed with Corinne and Hattie returning to the hospital every afternoon, but Michael had yet to show any signs of coming around. Their mornings were taken up with the making of practical arrangements in regards to medical insurance, arranging to stay on at the hotel and liaising with their tour operator about a later flight home, but in a way, that had proved to be a relief because it had briefly taken Corinne's mind off her situation. Their accommodation had been the least of her worries because, being January, the hotel had plenty of availability and the General Manager had readily agreed to them keeping on their rooms from week to week in the circumstances.

Sorting out the medical expenses had been far more complicated because, while Corinne being Corinne, had made sure they were well insured, there had been the matter of transferring funds out from the UK to pay Michael's medical fees in advance. She'd made daily update calls to Laura and Ben, who assured her that, with Annie in overall charge at The Oreford and the Cherringford, and with everyone else pitching in, they would be able to cope until she and Michael were safely

home. "You really don't need to worry about a thing," were her sister's parting words.
But Corinne did worry because it was now Friday and Michael had shown no signs of coming out of his deep sleep, as she thought of it. "I'm a pretty practical person, but honestly Hat, I really do not know how I'd be coping with all this without you," admitted Corinne, after they'd returned from the hospital and were having supper in the hotel's upper poolside restaurant.
"I found myself sort of in your position a few years ago when I was on a review visit to Kenya with a party of fellow journalists and I fell really ill and was hospitalised in Nairobi. We'd travelled up from the port of Mombasa on the famous overnight train and had been out to the Karen Blixen Museum, which is the centrepiece of a farm at the foot of the Ngong Hills made famous in the film Out of Africa, she explained. "Yes, that was a brilliant autobiographical piece about the Danish woman, who ran the farm wasn't it? But what happened to you?" Corinne asked.
"Whatever this bug was it was virulent and wasn't going away anytime soon, so as it was the beginning of the tour, the rest of the party had to go on without me. But one woman, whom I'd only known a few days, insisted on staying with me for as long as it took, which in the

end was the whole holiday. After that, I made myself a promise that if I ever found myself in a position to help a fellow traveller in trouble, I would also be there for them however long it took." There was a far-away look in Hattie's eyes as if she was reliving the experience. "So did you stay in touch with her afterwards?" asked Corinne. "We did for a couple of years, but she lived in Scotland, while I was in Dorset, and we were both leading busy lives, so we eventually lost touch with one another, which I do regret at times," admitted Hattie. "Well, we won't be losing touch, unless you want to that is. And when this nightmare is all over and Michael is well again, you will be welcome to be our guest at The Oreford Inn for as long as you like," she promised. "It would be nice to come and stay for a few days and I could write you a nice review for one of the out and about magazines to which I contribute," said Hattie. "They say that if one casts one's bread on the water, it will come back one hundredfold and I really do believe that you know." Said Corinne.

Back home in Little Oreford, it was supper time. Luke had turned up for the promised long weekend and Luca was already asleep in Lottie's old room. "So how have you been managing at the inns without Auntie Corinne and Mike?" Luke asked his dad. "Well better than expected, actually. While Annie, has taken overall charge, all our Old Mill House crafts people have formed a rota to manage our visitors' centre reception, which has left me free to be hands-on at The Cheringford," Ben explained. Luke hesitated. "Look mum and dad, I could always stay around and help for a few days." He'd been agonising over just when he should break his news to his parents and this seemed like the right moment. "Don't be silly Luke. How could you when you've got a home and career in London?" said Laura. "That's the thing Mum. I don't anymore! Now, there were tears in his eyes. It was as if everything had been building up to this moment's final reality check. "I've broken up with Roxanne, or rather she's broken up with me, I've quit my job and, if it's OK with you, I want to stick around here with Luca while I decide what to do next."

Chapter 19

George Simpkins pulled on to the M5 heading for Devon and Cornwall and was soon passing the turn off for the North Devon link road at Tiverton Parkway. It amused him to think that his enquiries had now taken him around in a giant circle, since that morning he'd pulled off at this junction on his way to meet Mark Hammond, a man, whom he'd decided, he did not much care for, although his wife had been charming. Still, if he hadn't met the hedge fund boss, he'd never have found his way to Little Oreford and one thing would not have led to another. Being January, there were plenty of hotel vacancies in St Ives and, having made a booking earlier that morning, he turned up at a Victorian pile called The Rocks, around four. 'This place looks like it might be on the rocks,' he thought, taking in the scene of faded grandeur from an earlier age, as he approached the heavy wooden reception desk in the lofty foyer. But the hotel was warm and the staff friendly. They had given him a large room on the first floor with a glimpse of the sea and, best of all, the bar served a good local pint and the food in the overtly plush and dimly lit restaurant was not at all bad. So, were the Jeffersons still in St Ives or had they moved on? That was now the question to be answered, he mused, as he carefully removed the tiny bones from the first of two kipper fillets, he was beginning to regret ordering for breakfast. George had a weakness for kippers, but he knew they'd be repeating on him for most of the morning. The easy thing to do now would be to go online and see if he could trawl through the town's electoral roll for Rachael and Anna Jefferson and for Rachael's parents.

But no, he preferred his tried and trusted way of requesting to see the copy held in the local library, or at the council offices. There he could usually find a helpful librarian, or clerk's assistant, willing to provide him with directions to a particular road or street. The library was busy with a queue of mostly older people waiting patiently to be served, although he'd noticed a self-service check-in and out facility available in the foyer. He joined the end of the queue, which thankfully did not grow any longer. With no one behind him, he hoped there would be no pressure, when he at last reached the first of the two librarians. She was young, so he moved smartly on to the second position, where the woman was far closer to his age and therefore would be more knowledgeable, he reasoned. She might have been more knowledgeable, but she was clearly not in a good mood that morning, telling him that as most everyone viewed the electoral roll on-line these days, they only had one copy and she would have to go and find it for him.

There were just under ten thousand people living in the seaside town and a slow finger running trawl down the long list of names eventually produced two Jeffersons, but not the family he was looking for. That was a bind because Rachael's parents had clearly both died and as she must have moved on. There was nothing he could do now other than go back to the hotel, get out his laptop with its keys faded from too much two-finger tapping and trawl back through the town's previous census records from, say 1990, to establish that Rachael's parents had indeed moved from Richmond to St Ives. But a frustrating hour later, he came to the reluctant conclusion that the family had probably never lived in the town.

Having found no evidence of their ever having been there, he could only conclude that they'd arrived and left again in the ten years between the censuses. There was nothing for it now, but to call on the town's other Jefferson families in the vague hope they might be related to Ivy and John, and to see if anyone at the school might have remembered their daughter Rachael and young Anna. 'I feel I'm running pretty close to the rocks myself at the moment,' he thought, returning to the hotel reception. He was just picking up another town map when his phone rang. "Oh! hi George. It's Sandy Loxton here from the paper. We've had a response from your appeal for information about the Jefferson family from a Miss Elizabeth Lyons, whose given me her number for you to call her. George thanked her. I owe you one," he said. "I could be free for a drink after work and possibly you might tell me a little about your work, off the record of course," she suggested. "That would be nice, but I'm down in St Ives, following another line of enquiry at the moment, so maybe another time," he replied. "That would be good," she responded before ringing off. He thought he detected a note of disappointment in her voice. George retired to one of the empty armchairs in the foyer and called the number. The woman who answered was clearly elderly with a cultured voice and listened in silence as he explained the reason for his appeal. "That's most interesting, Mr Simpkins. There are things I can tell you about the Jeffersons, so perhaps you might care to call in for a cup of tea around 4.30pm this afternoon," she invited. "Miss Lyons, I am extremely grateful that you have got in touch, but my enquires have since taken me down to St Ives and it

would be a long drive back to Glastonbury to see you," he explained.
There was a moment's silence as she absorbed the information.
"Which St Ives are you calling from Mr Simpkins, because there are two you know?" No, George did not know and was suddenly feeling put on the spot and highly embarrassed. "I am down in Cornwall," he admitted reluctantly. "Oh no, Mr Simpkins, because when the Jeffersons left Glastonbury, they moved to St Ives in Cambridgeshire," she told him. "How stupid and to think I regard myself as a private investigator, Miss Lyons," he replied. "Please do not be too hard on yourself, Mr Simpkins, because you're not the first to have made that mistake, so perhaps you will be free for tea after all." George said that would be most kind and, making a careful note of her address, promised to be with her later that afternoon. Coming off the phone, he rebooked the hotel he'd left the previous morning and called Sandy, telling her what had happened and arranging to meet her in the bar around 7pm. Twenty minutes later he'd hurriedly packed, checked out and was on his way back to Glastonbury.

Chapter 20

It had not been good news at the hospital. A specialist had come over from neighbouring Tenerife, especially to see them, and had expressed his opinion that Michael might well remain in his coma for weeks, or possibly even months, and in that case, perhaps it was now time to consider a repatriation to a hospital in the UK. Tests had shown there was brain activity and all the chances were that he would regain consciousness at some point and only then would they know how much, if at all, his mental and physical faculties had been affected.

"You know Hattie, I think I've known all along it was going to eventually come down to this," admitted Corinne. They were again having supper on the restaurant balcony overlooking their exclusive pool area. There were still a couple of guests enjoying a dip in the warm and balmy evening air, which only intensified Corinne's feeling of unreality. "I called Laura when I got back to my room to break the news and, do you know, she and my brother-in-law, Ben, are already more than one step ahead of me. They've been on the case and have made initial enquiries with one of a number of international air ambulance operators, who are highly specialised in repatriations to the

UK. Apparently, this sort of operation is happening all the time, which I guess isn't surprising really when you consider just how many millions of Brits fly off on holiday all the year around. It seems they will send a medical team out to assess whether Michael is medically safe to fly and, if so, then a logistics team will make all the necessary preparations and arrangements, including liaising with the hospitals both here and back home. So, I guess this is where we go from here Hattie," she said. "It's still all a horrible situation, but it must be a relief to know that all of this weight can now mostly be lifted from your shoulders," her friend pointed out. "I guess you are right," Corinne admitted.

Three weeks later on a damp and dreary February afternoon, a private jet carrying Michael and Corinne landed at Exeter Airport to be met by an ambulance, which took them both to a private hospital close to the city. Laura and Ben were at the airport to meet the flight and followed on to the hospital to collect Corinne.

There was much to discuss on the drive back up the M5 to Bristol Airport, where Ben was to pick up Corinne's car and follow them home to Little Oreford. But with poor Michael still in a coma, no one felt much like talking.

Once the two sisters were alone together, Corinne, feeling tired and emotionally exhausted, but now hugely relieved at being able to share her burden with Laura, let the flood gates open. She'd held herself together for Michael's sake, but now she just let herself go and wept. Laura pulled into a convenient layby, turned and hugged her until the emotional storm eventually passed. "I feel better now, so let's go home Sis," she said, drying her eyes with a tissue. It was on the way back that Laura told Corinne about Luke's split up with Roxanne and all the circumstances leading up to it. "Ben and I were pretty shocked and upset at first, but now we've come to terms with it and think it's probably for the best in the long run," she said. "So, what's he going to do now?" Corinne asked. "He and Luca are going to stay home for the time being and he's offering to lend a hand at either coaching inn or with the running of The Old Mill House. Luckily, they had room to take Luca at Hampton Green Primary, so I'm now fully re employed on the school run, taking and fetching him and the twins, while Lottie is pitching in and helping Ben out at The Cheringford," she explained. "I'm so sorry, Luke, has broken up with Roxanne, but I can't begin to tell you how grateful I am for all you and Ben have done to help me and Michael," said Corinne. "You don't have to thank us because I know you would have done exactly the same for us," her sister told her. They drove on in silence for a few minutes, locked in their own thoughts. "If Luke can help out at The Cheringford, that will be such a relief, as I plan to be at the hospital most days, just sitting and talking to Michael and doing all I can to help him come back to us," said Corinne. That is exactly where you should be and, as you can now see, you don't have to worry about a thing as far as the business is concerned. Oh! and by the way, Annie and Bob are accepting Alicia and Shaun's offer and going to live at The Woodlands when they go back to Toronto at the beginning of the summer holidays. Ben and I had another long chat with mum about moving back into the village, but she's definitely turned down the new apartment idea and says she will be perfectly happy without quite so much company at Little Oreford Court. We also broke the news to her about Luke and Roxanne and she suggested that if he and Luca were really going to be around for a while, then perhaps they might like to have a little more independence by moving into Lottie and Andy's old flat, which would be a bit more company for her," Laura explained. "That does seem like the perfect arrangement because he'd be able to keep an eye on mum, but what does he think about that?" Corinne asked. "I don't know, because she was going to suggest it to him herself when

he popped over with Luca to see her this afternoon," replied Laura.
"Oh! Gran, I seem to have made such a mess of my life, don't I?" There were tears in his eyes as they sat beside the fire while Luca played happily turning out the big wooden box of toys which Charlie always kept for the twins and for Olivia when Bob and Annie came around. He had managed to keep his feelings under control with his parents, but with his much-loved grandmother, it was different, as it had also been with Uncle Robin, whose loss he had felt more deeply than he had ever imagined he would. "No dear. You have not made a mess of anything. When you and Roxanne got together you both did what you believed to be right at the time, but often what was right then, doesn't turn out to be right later, and then you have to do your best to be brave and to adapt to new circumstances," she reassured him. "Oh! Gran. I know you are right. So was Roxanne right to break us up because she wanted us to take Luca and use my inheritance to go off and be hands-on with some save the rainforest project in the Amazon basin?" he asked. 'So that was what had broken their marriage.'
"I take it that you didn't think that was a good idea then?" said Charlie. "No, I didn't, because it made me realise

that if I did agree, then we'd most probably spend the rest of our lives chasing around the world on one climate fire-fighting mission after another and not really changing anything in the big scheme of things.
But having said that, I've quit my lectureship, where I really felt I was making just a small contribution to the younger generation's views on climate change and here I am back home again," Luke told her. "Yes, you are back home again because you have done the right thing in putting Luca's needs first. It would have been almost impossible to continue with your job while giving your son all the care and attention he needs. Now you have the strength and support of your whole family around you and time to take stock of your situation. You have all your Antarctic Survey and now lectureship experience behind you, so you will easily find a new position when the time is right," she pointed out. "Yes, I guess coming home was my only option at least for the time being," Luke conceded. "So, seeing that you are home for a while, why don't you and Luca move into Lottie and Andy's old flat, because that would give me the chance of seeing more of my great grandson and you a little more independence," Charlie suggested. "Gran, that's a great idea," said Luke.

Chapter 21

Miss Elizabeth Lyons lived in some style in a large house on the edge of Glastonbury. She was obviously a lady of substance, George noted, as he was led into her comfortable drawing room by a much younger woman, who was introduced as her companion, before withdrawing to make the tea. There was a log fire blazing and the central heating must have been operating at full capacity because George, sitting opposite the old lady in a sagging arm chair, was soon feeling uncomfortably warm and asked if he might take off his jacket. “It’s bitterly cold outside, but it’s nice and warm in here,” he said, taking out his notebook and pen before folding the garment and placing it neatly on the floor beside him. “I’m so glad you think so, Mr Simpkins, because I really do feel the cold you know. I guess it’s one of the small prices one pays for getting old.” George agreed, thanking her for getting in touch and asking how she might be able to throw some light onto his quest for Rachael and Anna Jefferson. If he didn’t get out of there pdq, he was going to cook and that was even with his jacket off! But Miss Elizabeth Lyons was in no particular hurry to see this handsome young man on his way, because he was young and attractive in her elderly eyes.

She began telling him all about her earlier life in the town, only interrupted by the arrival of the tea and delicately cut slices of sponge cake that tasted even drier than it looked. Eventually George, who'd done his best to listen attentively, could stand it no longer. Making an exaggerated gesture of looking at his watch, he apologised for having another appointment and would have to be leaving shortly, so what could she tell him about the Jeffersons?

"Oh, I am so sorry for rambling on, only it's so nice to have some interesting company these days. I got to know them while attending evening art classes many years ago. They were both extremely talented you know, but I think the daughter outshone her mother, especially when it came to watercolour. Anyway, I gave up because I soon realized I didn't have much talent, but we kept in touch after they moved to St Ives. That's the one in Cambridgeshire you know," she said with a twinkle in her eyes.

"We exchanged Christmas cards for a few years, but then that stopped," she explained. "So, you must have their address then," said George, his pulse quickening.

"Oh yes I do," she said, reaching for her address book, which she'd placed on the small table beside her chair.

Five minutes later he was out of there and on his way back to the hotel, having promised to let her know if he did eventually catch up with the Jeffersons. "What I need now is a shower," he muttered, realizing that his shirt was literally sticking to his back and he was meeting that helpful woman from the local paper in the bar in less than an hour.

Sandy Loxton had had one of those deadline days when everything goes wrong and was half wishing she'd not impetuously agreed to meet George after work. But the oak beamed bar with its subtle lighting, mellow furnishings and open fire suddenly relaxed her because this was traditionally a quiet time and there appeared to be no one around. It was like an oasis of calm and she suddenly felt the weight of the day slipping from her shoulders.

'What I need now is a large glass of chilled white wine,' she told herself, gravitating towards the oak panelled bar. "Excuse me, but are you Sandy?" a soft voice asked from the far side of the room as a tall, well-dressed man rose to his feet. "Yes, that's me and to be honest, I'm in need of a drink after the day I have just had," she said, coming slowly towards him, hand outstretched and with a smile on her face. "And I'm in need of one too having spent the last hour slowly cooking in a drawing room heated to a temperature that would have not been out of place in a tropical plant house!" George bantered. It was clear from the outset that he and this Sandy Loxton were going to get along, he thought, as he returned to their table with two large glasses of white wine. She was of medium height, he'd say some years younger than him, with cropped fair hair and a complexion to match and extremely attractive in his eyes. "OK tell me about your hot house experience," she said after he'd sat down and they'd clinked glasses. "No, you tell me about your day first," invited George, beginning to feel that this evening was certainly turning out to have possibilities. Sandy was half way through telling how their front-page story had to be changed at the last minute, after it was discovered to be a hoax, when the restaurant manager appeared with two menus, enquiring if Sir and Madam were going to be dining with them tonight. "Will you be my guest?" George asked. "I'd be delighted George," she replied. "The trouble is that we're both in professions where we're the ones, who like asking the questions, but we are not quite so keen when it comes to answering them," George observed when they were half way through dinner. They'd both made subtle attempts at unravelling one another's life stories.

He'd happily told her how he'd been engaged to find an attractive Costa Rican woman, who'd disappeared after attending a wedding in Devon and how one thing had led to another with his current assignment. But he did not mention his regular visits to Niece and was reluctant to say too much about his earlier life. "You're absolutely right George, I think that you and I are private people by nature, preferring to deflect attention from ourselves by asking questions to throw the spotlight on others," Sandy pointed out. She told him she'd closed the book on her life before moving to Glastonbury, some five years earlier, and did not really want to talk about it. He guessed she was probably ten years younger than he and it was very clear, she was very much her own person, displaying a high degree of independence. He was sorely tempted to probe her just a little further about her earlier life by sharing a few of his secrets, but decided that was not a good idea, not quite yet anyway. "It's been a lovely evening George, but I've had a busy day and I think it's time I was going, but I'd really love to meet up again," she said, after they'd both sent the sweet trolly on its way and finished up with a coffee. "Me too but in the meantime, I'll let you know how I get on in St Ives. That's the one in Cambridgeshire and not in Cornwall, you know."

Chapter 22

Corinne was driving towards Exeter on her way to see Michael, still grappling with her new bleak reality, when her hands-free phone rang. "Corinne it's me calling to ask if there's any news about Michael and if there is anything else I can do to help," Hattie asked. "Oh Hattie, you have already done more than enough, and I really don't know what I would have done without you. I'm on my way to the hospital now so I'll call you with an update later," she replied. "Look Corinne, I was due to fly off to South America for month, but that got cancelled, so I'm stuck at home here in Dorset, which is not a million miles away from you. So, I was wondering if I might take up your kind offer of staying at your Oreford Inn for a few days, while looking around the area, and maybe coming along with you to the hospital, her friend suggested. "Goodness Hattie, I'm going to be spending most of my time at the hospital, but if you'd really like to come, then, of course you can." She really liked Hat and having her around, if only for a few days, after they'd shared so much together, would be a comfort rather than a hinderance, she told herself.
Arriving at the private hospital, where all had an air of professional calm, she found that Michael had been

transferred to a spacious private room on the first floor, overlooking wooded grounds, and that a welcoming vase of fresh flowers had been thoughtfully placed on a side table. Taking off her heavy winter coat, she walked over to the chair beside the bed. "Hello darling, I've come to spend the day with you and I have lots to tell you about all that's been going on at home since we left," she said, fighting back her tears as she looked down on him.
He was all tube and wired up on his life support system. But his face looked calm and almost boyish, as if he'd relaxed into a deep sleep. Michael's new consultant, who introduced himself as Andrew Havers, appeared around noon to discuss the patient's on-going regime of care. He had a calm and gentle manner and Corinne felt instantly that here was a person in whom she could place her trust, to do all that he could to look after Michael until he regained consciousness.
She left the hospital around five, which was noon in Toronto, where Jonathan and Chrissy were just coming into the house having been out shopping with Sofia. The phone was ringing on the hall stand, so Chrissy answered it because Jonathan had his arms full of parcels and had gone on into the kitchen. "Do I have the pleasure of speaking to Miss Chrissy Morales?" Chrissy knew in an instant that this was her boss, calling from

the life she'd left behind. It had been a colourful and, at times, both exciting and frightening life, that she'd loved, and sometimes hated, in equal measure. It was a life of warmth and vibrance, so utterly different from that she was now living in fashionable and upmarket Toronto as the wife of a much respected and, she knew, envied lawyer. Yes, envied because she had seen the looks that colleagues and important clients gave her when they attended obligatory events in Jonathan's social calendar. Chrissy had thrown herself wholeheartedly into her new, safe and comfortable life and having Sofia had been her reward, but despite it all, there were moments when she missed her home country. "Carlos is that you?" she asked, knowing full well that it was. "Yes, it is and here I am sitting behind my big desk in San Jose and still waiting for you to send in your report on Senor Mark Hammond.

She could tell in an instant he was not being serious and that was a huge relief. "But instead of sticking to your duty, you met a Canadian called Jonathan Meyer at an English wedding and flew off back to Toronto where you married him and forgot all about your responsibilities to me and your team," he continued. "Carlos, it's good to hear from you after all this time and I did try calling you on several occasions to explain the situation and resign, but you were always out, so eventually I just wrote you a letter which you obviously never received. But how have you found out all this about me?" she asked. "That's easily explained. I just called up Sen Hammond and told him he was now off the hook, as far as his financial dealings with the former Jimarenal Corporation were concerned, and asked him if he would care to find out what had become of you. I could tell he was relieved and he willingly agreed to cooperate and it occurred to me that you'd probably upset him in some way and he'd relish the chance of paying you back," he told her. "I'm sure you are right about that," agreed Chrissy, instantly recalling the moment she'd turned her back on him at the wedding. "Anyway, sure enough, he called me two or three weeks later with your whereabouts, but how he found out I do not know," he said. A moments silence fell between them. "Just what did Carlos want? she wondered, feeling a small knot of fear beginning to tighten in her stomach. Knowing him so well of old, he would not have gone to all this trouble unless he wanted something. "It's lovely to hear from you, but why are you calling me after all this time? There was a pause as if her old boss was carefully considering his response. He'd had more than a drop too much to drink and was not actually behind his desk, but home in a small apartment block in downtown San Jose, having been let go several months earlier following a breakdown. “I felt we were pretty close at one time and, to tell you the truth, I could have fallen in love with you if I hadn’t been married with a young family,” he admitted, so I guess not knowing what had become of you started playing on my mind of late,” he told her. “So how are your wife and family?” she asked pointedly. “Ah, sadly, it’s the old, old story. I was spending so many long hours away from home that eventually she got fed up and took the kids back home to her mother, who never really liked me anyway,” he explained. “Oh Carlos, I am sorry and I feel guilty that you have gone to all this trouble to make sure that I was OK. So yes, I am absolutely fine and Jonathan and I now have a lovely daughter. I’d be telling a lie if I said I didn’t miss Costa Rica, so one day maybe we’ll come home for a visit and we could meet up and talk about old times. I’ve got to go now because I have food to prepare for lunch, but you can always call again if you like.” She could sense him hesitating as she was poised to put down the phone. “Look, there is one other small matter I would like to discuss with you concerning our closing down of the Jimarenal Corporation.” Chrissy knew she would be better off not knowing whatever it was that he wanted to tell her, but her curiosity got the

better of her. “You will remember that the old Godfather Edelmira Sanchez, had two associates, Antonio and Lucas, who’s sons Juan and Jose were also heavily involved in the corporation’s affairs and were each goaled for twenty years.
Well, Jose had a younger sister, Silvi, a very smart young lady with whom, against all the rules, I had a brief affair, while interviewing her. I know it was incredibly stupid of me, but things were not going well at home and my lust just got the better of me.” Chrissy could sense him pausing again, as if he was reluctant to go any further. “It turns out that Jose was able to transfer a sizeable chunk of the corporation’s funds to her in the days before he was arrested. He was probably tipped off that we were poised to strike, by some corrupt person high up on our side. Anyway, she now cruises the world on a superyacht, her command centre for anther international crime syndicate, which has risen from the Jimarenal ashes, and is partly controlled by her brother from beyond the prison walls!” he explained. “How on earth do you know all this Carlos and, more to the point, why on earth are you telling me?” she asked. “I know it because Silvi got in touch and told me several years ago. I think in some perverse way it was to punish me for what I did to her brother and knowing I would never

divulge the information for fear of her revealing our affair and destroying my otherwise spotless career. I've now been let go and chucked on the scrap heap, despite giving my life to our agency and my reputation is the only thing left to me," he explained, "So how do I come into this ugly frame?" she pressed, now wishing she'd put the phone down on him. "Because if something ever happened to me, I felt someone should know the truth about Silvi and the only person in the world I knew I could trust with my secret was you." A silence filled the two thousand three-hundred-mile void between them. "Look, Carlos, I feel honoured that you have shared your secret with me, but to be honest, it really is time for both of us to let all this go. We've had our day in the sun, so now it really is time to step back and leave it all to others. My life is here now. Yes, there are times when I do miss home, but I don't really think I will ever be coming back, so this should really be goodbye old friend," she said. "I guess you are right, but it's been nice to hear your voice again anyway," Carlos replied. Chrissy put the phone down, already feeling anger for that bastard Mark Hammond, welling up inside her. When Jonathan came back into the hall way, having dumped the parcels and got their daughter a snack, he heard Chrissy say 'Carlos.' It was not a name he

immediately recognised, but he was suddenly on full alert as memories of his frightening and uncomfortable time in Costa Rica with Corrinne suddenly surfaced.
"Who was that and what did he want?" he challenged.
"That, believe it or not, was my old boss, who'd somehow tracked me down through Mark Hammond, and how on earth that man knew where I was, I simply have no idea. He claimed that he'd never received my resignation letter and had finally gotten around to being concerned as to what happened to me after all this time. I told him and he wished me well and that was the end of it, so more importantly, what shall we have for lunch?" she asked in a feeble attempt to dismiss the call from their lives.
Although nothing further was said, Jonathan could not avoid the thoughts that kept on popping up from that uncomfortable and frightening time in his life. They'd hardly finished eating when the study phone started ringing and he hurried off to answer it.
"Hello stranger, so what's been happening on your side of the pond?" Jonathan greeted, pleased to hear Shaun's familiar voice. "I'm calling because I thought you should know that you're your cousin Corinne and Michael were involved in a nasty accident while on holiday in the Canary Islands and that he's been flown

home by air ambulance and is still in a coma in a private hospital." Jonathan was now on full alert. "Is Corrine all right?" he asked. "Yes, she and a woman journalist friend, in the car with them at the time, escaped with cuts and bruises. But Michael suffered a severe head injury and they don't know how long he's going to be in the coma, although the good news is that his brain activity suggests he will eventually wake up," Shaun explained. "That's a huge relief, but is it possible he might have suffered some paralysis as a result of the accident?" he asked. "Yes, apparently there is that possibility, but, of course, no one can tell at the moment. But there's also some good news because Annie and Bob have agreed to come and live at The Woodlands, which is a huge relief for Alicia."

Returning thoughtfully to the kitchen, Jonathan told Chrissy the news about Michael and Corinne, "I really think I should call her to see how she's bearing up and to tell her we're thinking of them both," said Jonathan.

"Yes, I think that would be a good thing to do," Chrissy agreed. She accepted that Corinne would always have a special place in his heart and because she loved him and she knew he really loved her, then why would she deny him his right to feel concerned. While he was on the phone, her thoughts returned to Carlos. No there was nothing for her now in Costa Rica and she doubted she would be going back, at least not for many years. Her mother had died from a drug overdose when she was four and she'd never known her father and had been brought up by grandparents, now both long dead. But it was Carlos's mentioning of the desk that she and fellow operatives had struggled to bring up from the ground floor that was now making her reflect on happier times Yes, there had been good times when difficult investigations had been brought to satisfactory conclusions and then there was the unspoken closeness she'd developed with her colleagues. She did occasionally miss the warm climate, her favourite local dishes and the chances to escape for a few days to Costa Rica's exotic Caribbean or Pacific coasts, just a short plane hop away, she thought, looking out over their large garden, locked in winter darkness. She had been a person in her own right, respected by her peers who knew that no one messed with Chrissy Morales! but now what had she become? 'Get real, would I really want to give up my wonderful new life for my old one?' she asked herself. Hell no, she thought, dismissing the question and going upstairs to put away the new winter clothes they had just bought for Sofia.

Corinne felt emotionally drained and quite physically tired as she climbed the stairs to the comfort of her apartment over the former stable block at The Oreford Inn, She had eventually run out of things to say to Michael and resorted to reading aloud the second of the two novels he'd chosen as his holiday entertainment, but had never opened. She had popped them into her holdall as an afterthought, After a while, she wondered if he might actually have had enough of her talking and she imagined him wanting her to stop, but having no way of asking her from the depth of his being.
"Yes darling, I will stop now," she told him, feeling certain this was how she should spend her days, talking to him through some veil that would eventually fade into consciousness. She was just stepping out of the bath after a long soak when her phone rang and she waited for the answerphone to kick in. She had no intention of answering it. But then Jonathan's still, oh so familiar voice, broke the silence and, grabbing a towel, she rushed to pick up the receiver. Asking him to hang on a moment, she quickly dried herself and then, lying propped up on her bed, which he had shared, she poured out the whole story from beginning to end. It was suddenly as if the years since they had parted had slipped away because dear Jonathan had always been a

good listener in a way that Michael never really was, which had irritated her at times. When at last she stopped talking and Jonathan had done his best to be reassuring about Michael's recovery, he told her about Chrissy's out of the blue call from Costa Rica and how Mark Hamond had found their contact details and passed them on to him. "I wonder just how he did that because we've heard nothing of him since Luke's wedding, not that we'd ever want to have anything to do with him again. But that'll certainly give me and Alicia something to talk about, because she's coming over for breakfast with Laura and I before I leave for the hospital," she told him.
When Jonathan returned to the kitchen, he thought he caught a faraway look in Chrissy's eyes as she finished packing their dishwasher. "A penny for your thoughts, as they say in the UK," he said. "Is that one of the sayings that Corinne taught you?" she countered.
Jonathan could see she was feeling upset because, despite her telling herself it was all right for him to talk to his former lover, the comment had just slipped out. "No that wasn't one of her sayings," he lied.

Chapter 23

Although it wasn't late when George Simpkins got back to his room, he decided that researching the St Ives, Cambridgeshire, electoral roll to see if Rachael and Anna Jefferson were still living at Old Willow Bank Cottage could now wait until the morning. Afterall, it had been a long drive up from Cornwall and he'd had quite enough for one day. He climbed into bed and began imagining himself slowly undressing Sandy, but within minutes he'd fallen into a deep sleep. He was woken around 9am by the sound of the traffic in the street below and with a slight headache, which he put down to the large nightcap he'd downed as a consolation prize after Sandy left. He hated getting up late because he always found the early mornings to be the most promising time of the day when all lay ahead and was to be played for. 'This won't do George, it won't do at all,' he scolded himself because, had he been up at his normal time of 6am, he'd have been one of the first down to breakfast and well on his way to St Ives by now. Instead, he was going to be playing catch up all day. But sod it. Why should he hurry and what was there to play catch up for anyway? It was not as if his clients were on his back because he'd heard nothing from them since they gave him their assignment, not like that pushy Mark Hammond, who was keeping his past life a secret from his attractive younger wife. Wealthy people like that were despicable in his eyes. No, he'd give himself a day off. He wouldn't bother getting out his laptop to see if the Jeffersons were still at Old Willow Bank Cottage until he got to St Ives.

That was the next stop on the roadmap of his enquiries anyway, and if he didn't get there until late, once he'd researched somewhere to stay, what the hell would it matter anyway? Sandy was also an early riser. That was normally essential when it came to her profession, in her view anyway, because being self-motivated and having a get up and go personality certainly made the job easier. But the day after the paper had been put to bed was her day off and now she was idly thinking about George and the good time they'd had together and how what might have happened if she hadn't made her excuses and left, because she was tired. 'Why not give him a call and invite him out for coffee?

No, he's bound to be well on his way by now,' she thought, glancing at her bedside alarm clock to see it was nearly 9.45am.

'Go on give him a call anyway,' her inner voice suggested. "George, I was just calling to thank you for a lovely evening and to invite you out for a coffee, but I expect you are miles away by now," she guessed. "As a matter of fact, I'm not. Under normal circumstance you'd be right, but I overslept and I'm just finishing my breakfast, so yes let's meet for a coffee later," he agreed. St Ives might have to wait until tomorrow now, he decided.

It was around the same time that Corinne, Laura and Alicia, later joined by Annie, were coming to the end of their breakfast catch-up in The Oreford's restaurant. Her and Michael's terrible accident had naturally been the main topic of conversation. But then Corinne told them about her long call from Jonathan and how Mark Hammond had somehow found their address. "Honestly, I'd thought we'd heard the last of that wretched man after Luke and Roxanne's wedding," said Laura.

But then, somewhere in the back of her mind, a penny dropped. Could it be only a pure coincidence that a private investigator called George Simpkins actually called into Ben's office just after Christmas, she told the others. "You mean, you think he might have been in the village making inquiries about Chrissy on behalf of Mark!" said Corinne. "And to think that we then went on and hired him to find Robin's Anna," she added. "I think it's possible it could be the same person and the only way to find out will be to ask him. I can do that as soon as I get home and find his card," she said, saying it was time she got back anyway. Annie took her cue, saying she should also get back to reception, leaving Alicia and Corinne together. "Do you fancy another coffee, only this is the first time we've had together for quite a while, unless you feel you should really be on your way to see Michael," said Alicia. "Yes, that would be nice," Corinne replied, suddenly feeling the need to tell her closest friend all about last night's conversation she'd had with Jonathan in more detail. "I know I should not be saying this, but I do sometimes miss him, even though I really do love Michael," she confessed. "If you can't share your innermost thoughts with me after all these years, then who can you share them with, other than Shaun," she pointed out. "Hmm, I don't think I could share that particular thought with him, now, could I?" They both saw the funny side of the situation and laughed. It was the lightest moment Corinne had experienced in weeks. "Dear Alicia, just what would I do without you?" she asked. "So, seeing it seems to be confession time, how do you really feel about leaving The Woodlands and moving over to Shaun's in Toronto with Anthony and Corina?" she asked.

"I know it's what both Shaun and Anthony want and I feel a whole lot happier now that Annie and Bob have agreed to move in and make our home their family home with Olivia. This will make it so much easier for me to come and go as I please, which Shaun says he will be perfectly happy for me to do," she explained. "So, you're going to turn into a right little jet setter then!" she joked.
"Who knows, it might be something like that," her friend replied. For a brief moment Corinne allowed herself to wonder if she and Jonathan would still have been together if she could have been more flexible, like Alicia was obviously now prepared to be. After all, running a small country coaching inn wasn't really that big a deal, was it? But no, on reflection, she would have been the proverbial fish out of water in his world, as he would have been in hers, and that, in reality, was the truth of the matter, she told herself. She could have gone on indefinitely with their trans-Atlantic arrangement, because it meant their lives had so much more quality and intensity when they were together, but it was he who'd had ended it all.
Ben was just leaving to go to The Old Mill House and then on to Cheringford to interview and new stand-in manager for the inn when Laura waylaid him with the news about Mark Hammond and the possible link with

George Simpkins, that she was now determined to prove or disprove with a phone call. “I’m not so sure that’s such a good idea because, even if it is true, he was just doing his job and if he hadn’t been doing it, then he would not be working for us now. I don’t see the point in challenging and possibly annoying him with your suspicions which may well not be true anyway,” he pointed out.

Sandy was waiting when George entered the busy High Street coffee shop, having just managed to grab a table in the window when a couple got up to leave. “We will have to stop meeting like this,” he said taking off his heavy dark winter coat and brown leather Stetson hat as he did so. He really was quite a handsome man, albeit looking a bit like he’d just stepped out of a Mafia movie, she thought appreciatively.

“I’ve just had a big idea I want to share with you and if the answer is ‘no,’ which I expect it will be, then that’s perfectly OK and you can forget I ever said it,” she announced, after he’d returned from the counter with their coffee. “Go on then. I’m all ears,” he replied, thinking that he really liked this woman and it would be quite difficult to refuse whatever she asked. “I happen to have a few days off now, so I was wondering if I might come along and help you in your search for the

Jeffersons. I think I'd find it fascinating, especially as I have also had to occasionally think out of the box and go looking for someone while out on a story. There now I've said it," she said, looking down and casually stirring her coffee. "I've certainly never had a request like that before and the answer is 'yes' on one strict condition and that is that you're not allowed to write about it under any circumstances. She nodded her head in agreement. "OK, so I guess I'd better call up and book a second room at The Golden Lion in St Ives, because that's where we're going to be staying tonight," he replied. "I guess you'd better had then," she answered, saying she'd pop home to pack a bag and would meet him back at his hotel in an hour. "Can this really be happening?" George asked himself as he strolled back in the cold winter morning sunshine.

It was fortunate he'd changed his car after completing his Mark Hammond assignment and was now driving a smart, nearly new, middle of the range, silver hatchback with a good turn of speed when required and that it had been thoroughly valeted prior to him driving it away. Sandy looked on approvingly, small overnight bag in hand, as he opened the boot and took it from her. "St Ives is quite a long drive from here, up the M5 and M4 and across country. So, we're not going to be there until around 5pm, allowing for an hour's late lunch break along the way, seeing that it's now past midday," he said conversationally as they headed out of town. "Fine by me, so why don't I make a start by accessing the town's last electoral roll to see if the Jeffersons are still at Willow Bank Cottage. That was the name you told me, wasn't it?" she said, reaching down and taking a small notebook and pen from her shoulder bag. "It was indeed," he replied, impressed by the fact that she'd remembered the address. But maybe first you'd care to choose a CD from the selection in the glove box," he suggested. "If there one in the player already, maybe we could start with that," she replied, now curious to know what the track might be. Without another word, he activated the player and Leonard Cohen's unmistakable voice suddenly filled the void singing 'Suzanne.' For some reason he was a singer, who had largely passed her by until he'd hit the heights with 'Hallelujah,' and then, out of curiosity, she had accessed his past albums. "Oh! so you're a Cohen fan, are you? and luckily me too, leastwise I'm a late convert," she said contentedly. They drove on in companionable silence. 'I can't believe this is really happening,' George said to himself for the second time that day.

“There are no Jeffersons living in St Ives anymore, so I’ll go back ten years, said Sandy, who’d volunteered to access the town’s electoral roll on her mobile phone. They’d been on the road for nearly an hour and were now on the M4 heading for London.

Leonard Cohen had just stopped singing, so he asked her if she’d like another CD. “Let’s have the one with ‘Suzanne’ on again because I think that’s my favourite album,” she told him. It didn’t take Sandy long to confirm that Rachael and Anna had been at the cottage at the time of the earlier census. “I’m getting the hang of this now, so shall we just rock up and knock on the door as soon as we get there to see if the current occupants know where they went?” she suggested. “No better to wait until tomorrow when we’re both fresh and besides, there really isn’t any hurry.”

Chapter 24

"Hello my darling here I am again," said Corinne, taking off her coat and hanging it behind the door. "I've got lots more news to tell you," she said, leaning over, kissing him on the forehead and taking her customary seat beside the bed. "First of all, Hattie's coming over for a few days and is arriving around four, so Annie has reserved our best room, which luckily happened to be free, and has ordered some fresh flowers from the florist in Draymarket. To be honest, I don't know what I would have done without her after our horrible accident. And to think how both our hearts sank when she suggested coming out with us, and we prayed that it would be a small car, so that it would put her off. Well at least that's what I was praying for. The not so good news is that Luke has broken up with Roxanne, or rather it sounds like she broke it off with him, so now he and Luca have come back to live with mum and he's going to be helping out in the business, at least until you've made a full recovery that is." She looked up, alerted by a gentle knock, to see Michael's consultant, Andrew Havers, and a colleague standing in the doorway with a nurse holding a clipboard. "I'll go for a coffee and come back a little later," she said getting to her feet. "We will only be a few minutes, but my office is at the end of the hall so please feel free to call in for an update if my door is open," he invited.

The small change in the tempo of the tiny sounds in the far distance was like a window opening in a corner of Michael's mind as it floated gently in a sea of nothingness and then all was silent.

But now those sounds were making themselves heard again and there was something in their steady, undulating rhythm that was familiar, but then they left him and the window closed. There was a coffee shop on the floor below with a comfortable lounge and seating area, reminding Corinne of one of those exclusive airport ones for VIP guests. But, there again, St Leonards Hospital was expensive and strived to make all its client feel like VIPs, she thought as she helped herself to a complimentary cappuccino.

Her phone vibrated in her pocket, because guests were required to turn off all their obtrusive ringing tones on entering the building. "Good morning. Is that Corinne Potter? Siegfried Summers here with the good news that the county planners have now approved your Little Oreford model village proposal in principle, as per our outline application. I've tried contacting Mr and Mrs Jameson, but they don't seem to be around at the moment. So, I am calling to ask if you would now like me to proceed to the detailed planning stage, as I know this exciting project was originally your husband's inspirational idea and he was extremely keen on making it become a reality". Corinne had completely forgotten all about the model village proposal, which in her heart of hearts, she did not think was such a good idea. Although she would never voice the opinion, she agreed with some of the older folk that it would attract thousands of visitors and start turning their small village into a theme park. But because it was Michael's idea and enthusiastically embraced by Laura and Ben, and indeed, the Rev Clark, she had decided to go along with it, but now she needed thinking about it like she needed the proverbial hole in the head.

"That is good news Mr Summers. I will let my sister and brother-in-law know and we'll get back to you," she said, deciding not to tell him about Michael, because that would only lead to a whole lot more questions, she did not have the desire, or the energy to answer at the moment. Andrew Havers' door was closed when she returned to Michael's room and again when she left around three, but had there been anything further to report, then he would have come and found her, she rationalized. Discussing the model village plan was the last thing anyone would want to think about in the current situation when they were all trying to cope with running the business without Michael. So, she'd leave it at least a couple of days before telling anyone about Siegfried's call, she decided as she drove home.

Hattie was just checking in with Annie when Corinne came in behind her, "Welcome to Little Oreford," she said, stepping forward and embracing her friend. "I'm sure you must be tired after your drive, so how about a cuppa in our residents' lounge, where I know there'll be a log fire burning, while your bags are taken up to your room," she suggested. "This is perfect and just how I imagined it would be," exclaimed Hattie, gazing around the cosy oak beamed room with its small leaded glass windows. "So that must have been a real blow having your Central and South American trip cancelled at the last minute," said Corinne, after they'd talked about Michael. "Yes it was, especially as we were starting in the Caribbean first, where it would have been quite a few degrees warmer than here. So have you ever been to that part of the world?" she asked. "I did spend a couple of weeks in Costa Rica a few years ago," said Corinne, deciding now was not the time to elaborate on that frightening experience.

"I hope it will be OK with you because I have arranged

for us to go over and have supper with my sister Laura and brother-in-law Ben, who are both very much looking forward to meeting you. Then tomorrow, I thought you might like to spend a little time having a look around the area, or you could come with me to see Michael if you wanted to, but honestly Hat, I don't mind which you choose," she said. "No question, I'm coming to keep you company and to see dear Michael."

Yes, Michael was dear to her,' she thought, as after an enjoyable evening spent with Corinne, Laura and Ben, she was climbing the stairs to her guest suite. She knew she was being watched by disapproving eyes as she'd struggled to get into her seat prior to their take off from Bristol Airport, but he had been the perfect gentleman getting up to help her. Then later in the flight, he had taken a real interest as she had gone on about all the places she'd been and the sights she had seen. She knew she was being a bore, but some inner need to impress drove her on as it had always done.

Chapter 25

It had just gone five pm when George and Sandy drove in to St Ives and checked in to The Golden Lion, in the heart of the small market town, and went off to their separate rooms to rest for a couple of hours, before meeting up in the bar for a pre-dinner drink. It had certainly been a whirlwind of a day, thought Sandy, as she undressed and climbed into the shower. When she'd asked George in the coffee shop if she could come with him, it had been half in jest and she'd not thought for a single moment that he'd actually agree. But he had and now here she was being his side-kick on the hunt for the Jeffersons. It was like the plot in some cheap novel, not real life. She was attracted to George and there was absolutely no doubt in her mind that he was attracted to her. He was at few years older than her, but that didn't really matter as far as she was concerned. So, what would the rest of the evening hold, she wondered as she dressed and prepared for her date. Yes, this in reality, was like having a second date with a man she really fancied. A few doors away, George was beginning to ask himself what he was getting into here because he knew this situation could really start getting romantically serious. The question was, did he really want it to and, if they did end up in bed together, which was now a distinct possibility in his eyes, just how would he feel in the cold light of the following morning? He was stuck in his ways, he knew that, and when he desired female company, all was neatly taken care of on his trips to Niece, where he enjoyed his other carefree life. If he and Sandy got together, all of that would go out of the window.

Then again, had he slightly miss read the situation, because she'd made quite a point about separate rooms? But maybe she would have done that anyway, because it was all part of the ritual dance, he rationalized. 'I'm in danger of over thinking this so why don't I go with the flow and just wait and see what happens?' he decided.

"Maybe it's time we knew a little more about one another's personal lives," Sandy suggested, after they'd spent an enjoyable evening comparing their likes and dislikes over dinner, and were waiting to be served with coffee. Both had been reluctant to talk about their past lives and loves, but now she saw no point in going on keeping secrets. "Fine by me, so ladies first as they say," invited George, deciding there and then that his other life down in Niece would not be coming into the conversation. "So where to start and how far back shall I go?" she asked. "That's entirely up to you," he said. "Ok so I've not always been a journalist. In fact, I only got into the profession some ten years ago when I bumped into an old university girlfriend, who'd launched her own womans' magazine and offered me a job. We'd been close at university, but had completely lost touch after going our separate ways, until that chance meeting, I was at a very low ebb at the time, having wrecked my life and just been released from prison!" George was suddenly on full alert, having only been half listening at the time, as a rather fine watercolour on the wall next to him had suddenly attracted his attention. "How on earth did you find yourself in prison?"

There, she'd come right out with it. because if she was going to have a relationship with an ex-copper and now private detective, then that was one secret that she could not possibly keep from him. Otherwise, it would remain like some pervasive shadow, never quite going away.

"I was an accountant with a quite large building firm, whose boss raped me at the annual Christmas party, when I'd had a little too much to drink. I should have gone straight to the police, but I really needed to keep my job, having spent ages trying to get one and besides, I was too embarrassed. He also had a wife, whom I really liked, and three young children, so I knew if I did report him, it would wreck their lives too." Sandy took a deep breath. "So, I decided not to get mad, but to get even, as they say, by syphoning off a little cash here and there when an opportunity presented itself, and it sort of grew into an obsessional game. But it came to an abrupt end a year later when he decided to sell the business and the buyers auditors came in to check the books," she explained, "How much had you taken and what did you do with the money?" George asked. "It was around £14,000, and that was the thing, I'd given it all to homeless charities. So, when it came to being sentenced, I was given six months because it was my first offence and I had not benefitted from what I'd done," she told him. "So, what did you say when you were asked to explain why you had taken the money?" George asked. "I just said it had become a game, which got out of hand, because I still didn't want to tell the truth and hurt that bastard's completely innocent wife, because if I had done so, it would have made all my past thieving kind of pointless, don't you think?

So, what do you think of me now George?" she asked. "Do you want me to be completely honest with you?" he replied, attempting to adopt a stern expression. "Yes, please George because I really don't want there to be any secrets between us," she replied quietly. "I think you are a girl after my own heart because I too have occasionally stepped outside the law when I felt it was justified and it's a real pleasure being in your company, so let me propose a toast. To my avenging angel," he said, raising his glass in salute. "Thank you, George, you can't know how much I appreciate that. So, shall we skip the coffee and go up to bed now?" They instinctively held hands as they reached the top of the stairs. "Your room or mine?" she asked. "In that case it's yours because it's the biggest and more comfortable," he replied. "How can you possibly know that when you haven't been into my room?" she challenged. "I do know that because I booked you into a suite, while I took a single room." Just how considerate was that, she thought, unlocking her door and leading him into her suite with its king size double bed. "Now I'm going to undress you and then I'm going to climb on top and have my wicked way with you," she announced, advancing towards him. "How can I possibly resist an invitation like that?" he said as they embraced and started kissing. Passion spent, they rolled apart and both quickly fell asleep.

'I think this has been just about the most exciting day of

my whole life' Sandy thought as she slipped into the other world of dreams.

Chapter 26

The vague sounds entering Michael's world were different from the earlier ones of which he had become vaguely aware, somewhere in the depth of his subconscious. But now he was hearing voices, familiar voices. It was if he had suddenly entered that relaxing state, somewhere in the limbo between sleep and dreams, having surfaced from the bottom of a dark pool of unimaginable depth. Michael opened his eyes to see first Hattie and then Corinne, but they were not looking at him, having been distracted by something at the large picture window he could see from the corner of his vision. What were all these tubes and wires he appeared to be hooked up to? What on earth was going on? "What am I doing here?" his vocal-chords responded in a barely audible whisper. "That bird must have flown into the window with some force to make a noise like that and I should imagine the poor thing has probably killed itself. But we can't really see from up here," Corinne was saying, as she turned and found herself looking straight into Michael's open eyes. Her heart leapt. "Michael," she uttered, moving quickly towards the bed followed by Hattie. There was a weak smile on his face, but then his eyes were closed again. Corinne was out of the room in

an instant and hurrying along the corridor to Andrew Havers' office door, which luckily happened to be open. "This is an incredibly good sign," he said, after he and two colleagues had finished examining new scans, taken later that afternoon and now revealing a near normal pattern of brain activity.
"Going on past experience, he will probably sleep for a few more hours now, so I would suggest that you go home and come back in the morning." If Corinne had been by herself, she would have insisted on staying by his side until he woke up, however long it took, but she did have Hattie to consider. "You can stay if you want to because I shan't mind in the slightest," Hattie assured her, but when the consultant pointed out that they could be there all night, Corinne decided that they would go home.
George and Sandy didn't bother rising early because the search for the Jeffersons had somehow lost its urgency and they were now far more interested in one another and their newly found intimacy. "So where did you spend your six months detained at her Majesty's pleasure?" He was resting with his hands behind his head as, passion satiated, they lay side by side. "Luckily, it was an open prison and, in hindsight, it was a fascinating experience, but not one which I would ever want to repeat, although I

might use it as the basis for a novel, if ever I get around to writing one. Anyway, you now know practically all there is to know about me, so now it's your turn," she countered.

"Not really much to tell actually. My older brother John and I grew up in a small house in North London, within earshot of the North Circular, mind you it was not nearly so busy in those days, and we both went to the local junior and senior schools. Our mum worked in a local grocery store and my dad was a plumber, who eventually drank and smoked himself to death after mum died of cancer. My brother joined the army and was killed in some stupid training accident and I joined the Met and rose through the ranks.

"But then I had an horrendous falling out with my boss and decided to resign and go off and paddle my own canoe, which as you know, I'm still doing." Now the moment of truth had come. Was he going to be as honest, as she had been, and tell her all about his other life in Niece and his relationship with Antoinette? No, this was not the time, he decided.

Leaving the Golden Lion around eleven, they made their way to the post office because, while they knew the Jeffersons had lived at Old Willow Bank Cottage, they had no road or street name to go with it. The woman behind the counter was relatively new to the town and suggested they call in at the sorting office next door where she was sure someone would be able to help. But the office door was shut and no one appeared in answer to their knock. “So, what shall we do now?” asked Sandy. “So now we either walk, or drive, around the town and find a postie and hope that he or she will be able to point us in the right direction, which is exactly what I did in Glastonbury,” he told her. “Oh! do let’s walk because I certainly feel I could do with the exercise after spending most of yesterday in the car, and besides, this looks a nice place to look around,” she said. “I would have thought we’ve already had enough exercise for one day,” he countered. “I’m going to ignore that remark,” she replied. Luckily, it was only fifteen minutes before they came across a postie’s distinctive hand pulled trolly parked beside a lamp post and he emerged from a gate opposite. Yes, he did know where the cottage was and that was a quarter of a mile away along a lane on the edge of town and far too far to walk from there. “Let’s hope someone’s at home,” said Sandy as they drove slowly along, looking out for a stone-built cottage set well back, according to the postie.

Continuing for some distance, they came to the conclusion, they must have missed the cottage and were making a three-point turn when a woman, walking a small dog, stopped to allow them to complete their manoeuvre. “Excuse me, but we’re looking for Old Willow Bank Cottage, which we’re told is along here somewhere, but we think we must have gone too far and missed it,” explained Sandy. “You haven’t missed it because it’s a little further on and I should know because I live there!” she told them with an enquiring look. She listened as George, now leaning across Sandy, towards the open car window, explained the reason for their mission. No, she’d never heard of the Jeffersons because the cottage had been empty for a couple of years and in terrible state when she moved in, she told them. “Now what do we do Inspector Clouseau?” Sandy asked. “His name was Jacques, not George, and what’s more he was a Frenchman, he retorted. “So now we drive back to the pub for a spot of lunch and a pint and then we make a tour of the local estate agents to find out who last sold the property and whether their records show who the previous owner was. And if we get really lucky there might even be a forwarding address. But Lady Luck was out that afternoon because no one, it seemed, could remember the last time a property of that quite distinctive name had come onto the market, let alone who the vendors might have been. “There’s one more lead we can follow, but it's a bloody tedious one and likely to be fraught with red tape," said George. They'd returned to the hotel, and were back on her bed, sitting against the padded headboard and nursing two mugs of tea they had just brewed. "And what is that?" she asked.

"I reckon Anna must have been of senior school age when she and her mum moved here, so that would have meant she'd have probably attended the local comprehensive, unless there's a private school around here. So, it's possible an older member of staff, perhaps an art teacher, might have remembered her. But there's so much security around schools these days that getting to talk to any of the teachers won't be easy, unless we collar them on leaving the premises," he told her. "That doesn't seem such a bad idea to me and at least it's something practical that I could do to help," she pointed out.

They were allocated the same table for supper and again George's attention was taken by the large watercolour of a beach scene, as they took their seats. "I love watercolours, especially seascapes, and this is a particularly fine one," he said, pointing the picture out to Sandy. "I didn't know you were interested in art, so if it's signed, perhaps I could purchase a copy as a gift for you

for allowing me into your life." Getting to his feet, George walked around behind their table to examine the picture at close quarters and then turned back to Sandy, "I'm finding this incredibly hard to believe it, but this picture was painted by an Anna Jefferson!" Sandy put down the glass of wine she was just raising to her lips, "You've got to be joking!" she retorted. "No, I'm not and it makes sense because one of the positive pieces of information I have picked up during my enquires is that young Anna was a talented artist. So maybe we can dispense with waylaying teachers with this lead to follow up."
"Can I assist you sir?" asked the restaurant manager, who had just come over to take their order.
"It may seem an odd question, but can you tell me where this picture came from and why it happens to be here in the restaurant?" George asked, "That's easy. It's a print and it was acquired from a gallery in Cambridge as part of a makeover by the hotel owners some years ago, and there are two or three similar ones along the upstairs corridors," he told them. "How do you know they came from this gallery?" Sandy interjected. "That's also easy madam, because there's a label on the back," the restaurant manager replied. "Would you mind if we took a look at the label later on when it's quiet, because we're rather taken with the picture and we might drive into

Cambridge tomorrow to see if this gallery is still selling this print or has a similar one?" George asked. "No be my guest, but more importantly, have you decided what you would like for dinner tonight?" he enquired. "Shall I let you into a secret?" Sandy asked, after their order had been taken. "And what might that be Madam Clouseou?" he asked. "I told you I went to university, but I did not tell you I was at Trinity College, Cambridge, studying economics and accountancy. So, seeing we're so close, I was rather hoping we might have a chance to wander around the old town and now we have the perfect opportunity," she suggested, "Sounds like a plan to me," said George, now beginning to think they were getting a lot closer to finding Anna Jefferson than he'd dared hope. Going in search of the other prints on their way up to bed, they quickly found the first on the middle landing and two others in small alcoves further along the corridor. They were smaller than the one in the restaurant, but equally exquisite, one being of an old rowing boat at the top of a strand of pure white sand, and the second of an old, flower garlanded, cottage beside a lane.

A fourth, on the wall opposite, was of a round stone castle on the shoreline between two islands and this was Sandy's favourite.

"If these were mine, I wouldn't keep them half hidden away up here," she said, taking pictures of the prints on her phone.

"What an amazing piece of luck, you being drawn to that painting in the restaurant and then finding the signature there," said Sandy, as they lay cuddled up in bed together the following morning and were just thinking about getting up. "Yes, it was, but I will tell you a curious thing and that is that, time again over the years, when I have thrown a lot of energy into an investigation, a point has come when a door has unexpectedly opened or help has come from an entirely unexpected direction and, don't laugh, I put this down to the power of positive energy," he explained. "I'm not laughing George because I've had a couple of similar experiences while chasing up on a story or suddenly coming up with a new feature idea right out of the blue," she replied.

Chapter 27

"You know, Hattie, and God forbid if I'm speaking too soon, I never really doubted for a single moment that Michael would come back to us," said Corinne, as they parked the car and were on their way into the hospital. A call earlier that morning had confirmed he had regained consciousness again around eight pm the previous evening and, although being a little confused and agitated, had quickly calmed down and remained awake for around an hour. Approaching Michael's room, they heard voices speaking in measured tones, so turned and made their way to the visitors' lounge. "I don't know about you, but I'm ready for a coffee," said Hattie, eyeing a tray of tempting looking pastries. But before they could help themselves, Michael's consultant entered and Corinne was on her feet in an instant and the smile on his face sent a tidal wave of relief through her entire being. "I am delighted to tell you that your husband is making a most remarkable recovery, the like of which I have not seen for a long time. He has had a thorough examination and, as far as we can tell at this stage, has not suffered any impairment of his physical or mental functions. He has now been taken off life support and you will be able to see him in about half an hour, I would say," he said, glancing at his watch. "Andrew, I can't thank you enough for the wonderful way you and your team have looked after Michael." Whether she should have addressed him so personally she did not know, but this was no time for protocol. "So, when do you think he might be able to come home?" she asked. "You must remember that Michael has been on his back for over a month and is quite physically weak.

We will need to build up his strength and get him walking again, so I think you should not be expecting to bring him home for a while yet, but all will depend on his rate of progress," the consultant explained. "Of course, how silly of me," said Corinne. "No, your reaction is completely understandable, Ms Potter."

Michael was sitting up in bed when they entered the room and broke into a broad grin when he saw them.

"Darling, you don't know how relieved I am that you've come back to me," said Corinne, sitting down beside the bed, taking his hand and dissolving into tears. Hattie, hovering at the door and uncertain as to whether she should enter, turned and slipped quietly away.

"It's all right my love. I seem to be OK, thank goodness, and I don't plan to go away again any time soon," he said squeezing her hand and waiting for her tears subside. "Do you remember the accident?" she asked tentatively, reaching down into her bag for a tissue and drying her eyes. “Do I remember the accident?” he asked himself, as if repeating the question would somehow invest it with more relevance. “Yes, I seem to, but remind me what happened because the medics here have not been terribly forthcoming,” he told her. “We were on holiday in Fuerteventura and had left the hotel with Hattie and a guide for a day’s sightseeing tour when we were hit by a lorry careering down the road out of control. We were pushed off the road and rolled down a steep slope before landing upside down against a large rock. You were knocked unconscious, but Hattie and I escaped with cuts and bruises,” She didn’t mention the guide and Michael did not ask so she decided to leave that until another time.

There was a tentative knock and Hattie put her head around the door. “Here comes our guardian angel and I don’t know how I would have managed without her,” said Corinne.

Chapter 28

George and Sandy drove into Cambridge and parked up on a long road running parallel to the old town with its spires now visible some distance away across a wide tree fringed green. “This is all just as I remember it and this is what they call The Backs,” she said, taking his hand as they strolled across the grass towards the River Cam, now separating them from the city. “Later this afternoon we could hire a punt and you could try your hand at being a gondolier,” she suggested, knowing full well that George had confessed earlier that he had an aversion to anything to do with boats and the sea. “Let’s find this gallery first and do our sightseeing later, but I won’t be going anywhere near any punts,” he declared. The narrow street winding its way through the old town and bordered by hallowed college entrances, was thronged with students and tourists. The first young woman they stopped, as she wheeled her bicycle towards them, knew where the gallery was to be found and directed them towards it, “This is certainly a place for wealthy tourists,” George noted as they stood peering through the window at oil paintings in heavy gold frames mounted on heavy easels. “Not the sort of place one would expect to find prints of seascapes for sale,” he

remarked as they pushed open the heavy glass door with its polished brass fittings. The lofty showroom with its old wooden floors, displayed a large collection of fine quality original watercolours of every description at prices from circa £600.
"Now that's what we came here to find," he remarked, as they wandered through into a smaller room featuring seascapes and beach scenes very like Anna's work.
"Can I be of any assistance?" asked a smartly dressed woman, suddenly materialising beside them. "Yes, you may be able to help because we are looking for works by watercolourist Anna Jefferson, aren't we," he said turning towards Sandy. "Oh Anna, yes she is one of our most sought-after artists, but sadly we have nothing of hers in at the moment." The explanation was sweet music to their ears, "That is a shame, but I don't suppose you have any of her prints for sale," George asked casually. "Unfortunately, no, sir. We have the exclusive rights for the sale of Ms Jefferson's work and we stopped producing prints a few years ago," she explained. "Ah! in that case, might you be able to supply us with a telephone number, or perhaps an address, so that we might write to her?" George suggested. "Oh no sir, we are not in position to divulge such personal information because of data protection, as I am sure you

must be aware," she pointed out. "Ah yes, of course, data protection," George repeated. "Can I be of any assistance?" asked a dapper man, sporting a dark waistcoat, matching trousers and expensive open neck shirt, who was clearly the gallery owner. "I'm hoping so," said George, producing the business card he always kept handy in a breast pocket for such occasions. "My name is Simpkins. I am a private investigator and my colleague and I have been charged by a firm of solicitors to ascertain the whereabouts of Miss Jefferson, as they have some business to discuss with her. So might I prevail upon you to contact your client and ask her if she might find a moment to get in touch?" he asked. "I will do as you ask, but Ms Jefferson is an extremely private person, so I could not guarantee you will get a response," he replied.

"Perhaps writing her a letter for us to forward might produce a more positive outcome," he suggested. George agreed that it might and thanked him for his help, "Daphne will you kindly supply Mr Simpkins with one of our business cards?" he instructed, before excusing himself and turning away to attend to another couple who had just entered the gallery. "Will you give him a letter George?" Sandy asked, as they stepped out into the sunshine. "Maybe, although it will be a last resort, but come on, I'm hungry so let's go and find somewhere to eat. All the cafes along the main street were busy and all the pubs and bars rammed with students, but they eventually found a quiet corner in a centuries-old inn called The Bear, some way from the busy town centre. Sandy got out her phone and started casually thumbing through the shots of all four of the hotel's prints she had taken. George had gone to get their drinks and pick up a bar menu. "I wouldn't like to meet him on a dark night," he said, glancing back over his shoulder as he stood over her with the drinks. Looking up and following his line of direction, she too spotted the life-sized brown pair standing up on his hind legs with his paws outstretched. "No nor would I," she agreed, turning back and picking up her phone. "Look George I've had an idea," she announced. "That's good because I seem to be running out of them," he said, picking up his pint and taking a first welcome sip. "So, here's the picture of that castle, which is actually more like a round stone tower sitting on the shoreline between two small islands. It's a pretty distinctive landmark, so if we can find out where it is, then we'll know that's where Anna was when she painted it, or just still might be now," she reasoned.

“All her paintings seem to have a remote island quality about them,” don’t you think,” she added. “Hell, Sandy. I really think you might be onto something,” said George, feeling that familiar rush of excitement he always experienced when he knew a break-through was close! So, islands, now just where and when had he been thinking about islands over the past few weeks or months? Then it came to him. Of course, it was over supper on that first night in Glastonbury when he’d wondered where New Grimsby was because it was the rather unusual name of the villa where Rachael and Anne Jefferson had lived. He’d looked it up only to discover it was not in the New World, as he’d assumed, but in the Isles of Scilly off the tip of Cornwall. “I think I just might know where that castle is Sandy and that’s in the Isles of Scilly. So why don’t you give their tourist office a call and describe it to them?” he asked. “I’m on it boss,” she said, picking up her mobile.

Chapter 29

Michael remained in hospital recuperating for another ten days while being visited by Corinne and Hattie, and on separate occasions by Laura and Ben and Annie and Bob with Olivia, and also by Luke, who'd left Luca with Laura. "I'm really sorry to hear about your situation Luke," said Michael, after he'd finished the routine of telling all his visitors about the progress he'd made since recovering consciousness and how he was feeling. "I know, I really didn't think for one moment it would all end up like this, but I guess having Luca was the mistake, which was really of my own making. I knew she wasn't the maternal type, yet I persuaded her it was a good idea. I thought that having a child needn't necessarily, get in the way of our campaigning work, which of course in the end it did. That was entirely my fault because, while she would happily have disappeared off to the Amazon basin with Luca on her back, when it came right down to it, I was not, and I can't really blame her for that," he admitted. "No one's to blame Luke. It's just one of life's experiences we all have to go through, and hopefully learn from. So, what's the situation now?" he asked. "We're selling our property, which her father helped fund, and she's keeping the proceeds. But she says she'll only take a third of Uncle Robin's legacy, when we eventually receive it from Claude, and not the half to which she's actually entitled because I'm going to be the one wholly responsible for bringing up our son, so I guess it's fair," he conceded. "Did you part on amicable terms Luke?" Michael asked.

"It was pretty stormy at first, but in the end, there was more sadness than anger," he said. "So, what are your plans now because your aunt tells me that you've been helping your dad out at The Cheringford and that you'd be happy to help me when I get back on my feet?" said Michael. "That's right and if you and Corinne and mum and dad do go ahead and get planning permission for the new model village, then I thought that perhaps I could oversee the project and go on to manage it," he suggested. "You've certainly got my blessing on that one, but what about your lecturing and all your campaigning on climate change?" asked Michael.

"That's still important, but Luca is my priority now and must be for the next few years at least," Luke replied.

"Hello you two," said Corinne, entering the room and coming over to take the chair on the other side of the bed.

"I come with instructions because your mum wants you to call in at The Allway Centre on your way home and

has given me a grocery list so here it is," she said. "I guess I have my marching orders then, but it's time I was going anyway," said Luke, getting to his feet. "I've made an executive decision," Corinne announced once her nephew had left the room. "And what is that my love?" she asked. "I've suggested to Laura and Ben, and they have agreed, that we put the B&B business at Rose Cottage on hold and move back in there again ourselves so that we have a separate home of our own, at least for the time being, rather than go on splitting ourselves between mine at The Oreford and yours in Wixton," she told him. "I can't say 'no' to that," he said and then pausing for effect. "Especially as Mr Havers has given me the all clear to go home tomorrow!"
"Thank goodness for that, so now we can put this whole nightmare behind us and move on with our lives," said Corinne.
"Yes, back to the grindstone after all these weeks of lazing in bed and being pampered by everyone!" he joked. "No, not back to the grindstone, because this whole horrible experience has been a real wake-up call and I'm determined to find ways of making our lives a whole lot easier from now on," she vowed.
"That will certainly be OK with me, so what have you and Hattie been up to?" he asked. "She took herself of to

Lynmouth yesterday and is planning to leave tomorrow, but she sends you all her love and has already booked to come back and see us all again in August," she told him. "That's OK then, but on a completely separate subject, which I suddenly began thinking about when I woke in the night, what has happened about that private detective being commissioned to see if he could find Robin's love child?" he asked. "Ah yes, Mr Simpkins," said Corinne. "It was left that he'd be back in touch when he had some positive news one way or another. But we've not heard from him since and, to tell you the truth, what with our accident and everything else that's happened since, I guess no one has given that a thought". She paused "Well that's not quite true because Laura reckons that when he called in to see Ben at The Old Mill just after Christmas, he was actually on another assignment to find out what had become of Chrissy on behalf of that rotter Mark Hammond, whom she dumped at Luke's wedding. Laura wanted to call him up and tackle him about, But Ben advised against it, so she took his advice.

Chapter 30

Back in Cambridge, George Simpkins was half way through his second pint and now on full alert as Sandy had just got through to the Isles of Scilly Tourist Information Centre at her third attempt and was beginning to describe the round tower, to the woman who answered her call. “No need to go any further because that’s Cromwell’s Castle on Tresco, just across the narrow channel from neighbouring Bryher,” she replied. ”Are there, by any chance, any artists living on Tresco?” Sandy asked tentatively. She got a thumbs up from George because that was the next question he would have asked. “There are quite a few artists on Scilly with their studios dotted all around the five inhabited islands, but whether there are any on Tresco at the moment, I really could not tell you,” the woman responded. “Ask her if she’s an islander, and if so, whether she’s heard of an artist called Anna Jefferson,” George instructed. Sandy rolled her eyes. “You forget I’m a journalist and I spend my life asking relevant questions,” she retorted. No, she was not an islander and had never heard of Anna Jefferson. “But the artists’ community on Scilly is pretty close-knit so if you call one of their galleries and enquire if they know an Anna

Jefferson, I'm sure you'll get an answer," she suggested, saying she now had to go because there were others requiring her assistance. Five minutes later they had confirmation that an Anna Jefferson was indeed living on the main island of St Marys, but worked from home and, better still, they now had her address!

Strangely, Sandy's jubilation quickly dissolved into disappointment with the realisation that the mystery, which had brought them together, had suddenly been solved and that their quest and journey together would soon be coming to an end.

"So, I suppose that's that then," she said, dejectedly.

George picked up on her vibe instantly, because it mirrored his own feeling of disappointment. "Well not unless you want it to be. I know we could end this adventure right here and now with a call to the Jameson family. But my gut feeling tells me we should see the thing through by taking ourselves off down to Scilly and going to meet Anna. After all, there may be reasons why she might want to leave the past in the past and not suddenly have it thrust upon her. I think we have a duty to give her that choice, don't you?" he said. "Yes, I do George, I really do, so shall we get it all sorted out here and now?" she asked. "I don't see why not because this place is open all day and its nice and quiet and I don't think that bear will disturb us." Luckily there was a flight to Scilly from Land's End to the main island of St Marys at 3pm the following afternoon, which they booked straight away, and no shortage of accommodation, seeing it was out of season. "I rather fancy that Star Castle Hotel because it's a castle and it was Cromwell's castle that led us to the islands in the first place," said George. They spent the remainder of the afternoon sightseeing before driving back to The Golden Lion for supper and an early night. They checked out around 7am and made the airport with plenty of time to spare. "George, this is beautiful. I'm so glad we came," said Sandy, squeezing his hand as, looking down on a myriad of islands caught in the golden winter glow of a late afternoon, their Skybus light aircraft began its descent into Scilly. The hotel had sent a taxi for them and, some twenty minutes later, they had driven down from the airport, through Hugh Town, and up to the small star shaped Elizabethan castle on Garrison Hill. "This is simply breathtaking said Sandy as, climbing out of the taxi, they turned to look out over the busy harbour, awash with moored launches and other small craft, and then across the water to the nearby islands. "And I've certainly never stayed in a castle before," he replied, as they turned and went inside. "Your room is up on the first floor and I have taken the liberty of booking you in for dinner, if that's OK, because you won't find much choice down in the town at this time of the year," the helpful receptionist explained, as they stood at her small desk in the heart of the castle, "What an amazing place this is," said Sandy looking about her. "Yes, it is rather special and we even have a Dungeon Bar if you fancied a before dinner drink," she added.

"We seem to have come quite a long way together since you called me at the paper about an appeal for information. I'm due back at work in a couple of days, so I guess the question I am now asking is where do you and I go from here George?" They were lying on the bed having just made love, following an excellent dinner and probably a drop more wine than intended.

"Well, I guess I should ask you in return, where you would like us to go from here?" he countered.

"We are from completely different worlds and have very different lifestyles and I am not quite sure how we could combine them, other than embarking on a separate homes, weekends and holidays relationship, at least for the time being," he suggested. "George that would suit me just fine, because I'm not really someone who needs to be in a live-in relationship and I think you are the same. So, if you'd be happy with that kind of arrangement, then so would I, but no playing away because that would be against the rules," she told him. "No playing away," he agreed, wondering how he'd feel when he next felt the need to fly off down to Niece. But then again, he could now take Sandy with him, provided he was upfront about his previous attachment to Antoinette.

Old Stones Cottage was tucked away in a large garden, just a short walk around the coast from the harbour and the old lifeboat station. They had found it easily enough having gone into a gallery and asked directions from a fellow artist, who just happened to be in at the time. "So here we are then," said George, as they hovered uncertainly outside the gate, peering in to a wild and rambling garden, which looked like it would become a riot of colour come spring and summer. But Old Stones was certainly no cottage, more a substantial two-storey villa with a pitch slate roof and long shuttered windows on both the ground and first floor. Walking uncertainly along a gravel path, they turned a corner to come upon a substantial pillared dark blue front door with a large brass knocker and mercifully also a bell.

George pressed it once for several seconds and they heard it ringing somewhere deep in the house.

He was about to press it again when they both became aware of a movement as a young woman appeared from along a side path. "Can I help you?" she asked. "Yes, we are looking for Anna Jefferson," said George. "Then look no further because my mother is working in her studio," said the young woman, who had the air of a student about her, and started leading the way across the lawn to a set of stone steps, half hidden in a hedge. They followed her up and out onto a small, grassy plateaux with views over a sandy beach. They turned to see a large Victorian summerhouse with doors flung wide open to capture the light.

"Mother you have visitors," the girl announced, as George and Sandy, hovering uncertainly at the entrance, peered in to see a woman, probably in her early fifties, with striking red hair, sitting at an easel. "Do come in won't you, as I assume you have taken the trouble to come all the way down here from Cambridge," she told them. "Yes, indeed that is the case," George confirmed. "So, may I introduce myself? I am George Simpkins and this is my colleague, Ms Sandy Loxton, and I guess the gallery may have already told you, we have been trying to contact you on behalf of clients, who have something of importance they wish to discuss with you," he explained. "They did indeed, Mr Simpkins, and I was wondering when you might show up and here you are. So, are you at liberty to disclose the nature of this business?" George paused, now wondering just how far he should go and what he should leave in the hands of the Jameson family. "I think, I can go no further, other than to tell you that it concerns your recently departed father, Robin Anthony Lloyd, and that I am making this enquiry on behalf of Laura and Ben Jameson of Little Oreford in North Devon, who were his long-standing friends."

Anna Jefferson put down her paintbrush and just stared at them, clearly overcome with shock. "Are you all right mother?" her daughter asked, hurrying to her side. "Yes, I will be in a moment Josie," she replied, making an effort to pull herself together. "I do apologise for springing this momentous news on you, but as you asked, I could see no other way this could be done," said George. Taking out his notebook and tearing out a page, he wrote down the Jamesons' address, telephone number and email, and handed it over to her. "Would you care to stay for coffee because I am intrigued to know how you found your way to me in this quiet part of the world?" she invited. "That would be very kind of you, but, in truth, being a former policeman, it was very much a combination of routine detective work and luck in coming across some of your lovely watercolours," he explained. "Now I'm even more intrigued, so Josie, why don't you take our guests into the house and make the coffee while I finish up here," she suggested. "I warn you now that mother's finishing up can take quite a long time, so you might well have had your coffee and gone on your way be the time she puts in an appearance," Josie warned them. She led the way into a traditional Victorian style conservatory behind the house and through into a large square kitchen. "If you'd care to see some of mother's paintings, then there's a fine selection in the drawing room at the end of the hall on the left," she said, putting four large mugs on the kitchen table and beginning to make the coffee. "I'd love to take any of these pictures home, especially that one called Hell Bay on a Stormy Day. So, I wonder which island that one's on," said Sandy.

"That's one of my favourites too and it's on Bryher," said Anna, now standing in the doorway. They followed her back into the Kitchen. "So, Anna, I know you're intrigued as to how we found you, but might I start by asking how you came to live on Scilly because I suspect that maybe your great grandparents were islanders," said George, when they were all seated around the kitchen table.

"How perceptive of you, Mr Simpkins, but what on earth

led you to that conclusion?" she asked. "The only piece of information I had to go on at the beginning of this investigation was an address, that being New Grimsby House in Glastonbury, where you stayed as a child, and, of course, when I looked it up, I discovered that New Grimsby was a harbour on your neighbouring island of Tresco. People often name houses to remind them of places, for which they have, a special attachment, so it followed that perhaps the former owners of New Grimsby House in Glastonbury, felt something special about the Isles of Scilly. I know it was a slender clue to go on, but when one only has an address, one has to consider every possibility," he told her. "You are absolutely right because my forebears were among the first tourists ever to step foot on Scilly. They took passage with an enterprising Captain Tregarthen, who made his living ferrying supplies to and from the islands, and they liked it here so much that they decided to stay," said Anna.

"So, to cut a long story short, we eventually traced you and your mother, Rachael, to St Ives, where we stayed at The Golden Lion, only to spot a watercolour print of Cromwell's Castle on Tresco by one Anna Jefferson. The picture had the Cambridge gallery's label on the back, so need I say more," said George.

"That is still all pretty remarkable, Mr Simpkins, and if ever I need a private detective, then I'll be knocking on your door," said Anna. "I think perhaps it's time for us to take our leave, so might I ask if you will be getting in touch with the Jameson family because that is your right to decide? If you do not wish to be found, then I will tell them so," he assured her. "That is very noble of you George, if I may call you George, and, yes, I think Josie and I will be getting in touch in due course, so you have my permission to pass on my details to them. But before you go, Ms Loxton, might I make a gift to you of that picture of Hell Bay which you so admired?" she asked. "That would be simply amazing and so generous of you, but only if you are really sure you want to part with it," said Sandy. "I am quite sure because it will give me a golden opportunity to go over to Bryher and paint the scene again," she said. "In the meantime, we'll have yours parcelled up and sent to you if you would like to give Josie your address," she added.
"Well mission accomplished, and now you're the proud owner of an Anna Jefferson original that's got to be worth circa £600, judging by the prices in the gallery," said George. as they walked slowly back to the castle. "It's our picture George, not mine, but perhaps I could

have it for safekeeping for the time being anyway," she suggested. "Sounds like a plan," he replied

Chapter 31

It was now three months since George had called Laura to give her the good news, together with Anna Jefferson's contact details. He readily admitted it was he, who, acting on instructions from Mark Hammond, had come to Little Oreford in pursuit of Chrissy Morale. Laura assured him they had absolutely no issue with that, other than to say that for reasons she'd rather not go in to, Mark Hammond. had now sunk to new depths in the family's estimation. Laura and Ben wrote to Anna introducing themselves and saying they were content to wait until she was ready to get back in touch. However, when she did so, then she would be most welcome to come and stay at Their Oreford Inn, originally acquired by her late father and her aunt Margo and finally transferred to the Jameson Family Trust.
It was a Sunday afternoon at the beginning of April and they were just beginning to wonder whether or not to contact Anna again, when she finally called. She said be delighted to come and meet them and to take up their very kind offer of staying at The Oreford Inn.
"Life with my mother was never easy," she explained, after everyone had gathered to meet her over lunch at Albany House.

“I never doubted for one moment that she loved me, but it always seemed to me that, wherever we were, then she wanted to be somewhere else. Consequently, we were always on the move and no sooner had I settled in one school and started making friends, like I did in Glastonbury, then I was taken out and I was on my way to another.

You asked me how she supported us and the answer is that I really don’t know, other than to say we never appeared to be short of money and she was always extremely well dressed. Mother seemed to have a lot of friends, always ready to put us up for weeks on end without question, during which time she'd disappear dressed to kill for a few days, although I was never told where she went or what she did,” explained Anna.

“So do you remember the day she took you to see your father?” asked Charlie, who could contain her curiosity no longer. She was sitting at the head of the table, feeling like the grand matriarch she indeed was, surrounded by her two daughters and their husbands and her grandchildren, Luke and Lottie and Lottie’s husband Andy. Her great grandchildren Jack and Hannah, being charged with looking after little Luca, were all in the lounge engrossed in a film on the television. “Yes, I do remember that day,” Anna replied.

"But she never told me Robin was my father. I remember it distinctly because it was the first time she'd taken me into London on the train and we'd ridden on the underground to his house, which was a real thrill. We were only there a for a few minutes before going to see Buckingham Palace and then we had tea on the train going home. I can't have been more than four at the time, but my memories are as sharp as if it had been yesterday." Her mobile started ringing in her bag beside her and she glanced down at it uncertainly. "Do you mind if I answer this because it will be my daughter, Josie?" "She's studying art and design at Exeter and is planning to join us tomorrow, if that's still all right, Laura." Sitting quietly beside his sister, Luke was now on full alert.

Mum hadn't mentioned that Anna's student daughter was also coming to stay! The conversation lasted for a couple of minutes.

"Oh! your car's broken down and you'll be needing someone to come and pick you up from Tiverton Parkway," she said, looking around expectantly at her hosts for an answer. "That's not a problem, Mum, because I'd be happy to nip down and pick her up," Luke volunteered. "Problem solved then," said Ben, smiling at Anna. "So, after leaving Glastonbury, where you were really happy, and then moving on from St Ives, what happened next?" he asked. "Next, we went to live in a large country house in Hertfordshire owned by the Frys, who were distant relations of my mother's, and there at last we settled down. He was a retired banker with limited mobility and walked with a cane and she wasn't in the best of health. So they really welcomed us in, as they had no children of their own, and mum and I sort of settled into a caring role. I think by that time, even mum had finally tired of always being on the move and as we were now living in a fine a country house with a gardener and a cook, she was as content as she was ever going to be. I went to the local senior school and then on to art college in Hampshire and from there I joined a fine arts publishing company. Mum remained living with the Frys and gradually took on running the household, while becoming passionately interested in the gardens. But then, sadly, she developed a particularly virulent cancer and died within six months. The Frys, who were really no longer able to cope by themselves, sold up and moved to an expensive retirement village, which had recently opened close by and where I visited them as often as I could until they both eventually passed away, leaving me financially independent.

By that time, while I enjoyed the fine arts world, all I really wanted to do was to paint and what better place could I think off for a base than in the idyllic Isles of Scilly," she told them. "There was a watercolour of the Tresco Gardens on the wall when we lived at New Grimsby House in Glastonbury and for some reason it really captured my imagination. So, I moved to St Marys, where I was eventually able to adopt Josie after her parents tragically drowned in a sailing accident. Bringing up my darling Jose while opening my own gallery and selling my watercolours, has given me a most wonderful and fulfilling life. Then a few years ago, a Cambridge gallery owner and art dealer on holiday, saw my work and offered to promote me on the mainland. I agreed and it was he who called me back in February with the news that I might be receiving a visit from a private investigator, and so there you have my whole life story," she said, smiling around at them all.

Chapter 32

That afternoon the family strolled with Anna across the green to Robin and Margo's cottage, where Lottie and Luke showed her around and took her out into the gardens where, as excited children, they'd first set eyes on 'Uncle Robin's' model village.
From there the family made their way to St Michael's and to her father and Aunt Margo's grave, which Lottie had planted around with spring flowers. Gazing around the peaceful country churchyard, Anna spotted a seat beside a path and amid the trees and said she would like to sit there for a while and would join them back at Albany House later. When she returned, Laura and Ben showed her into the lounge where tea had been laid out and all the family had reassembled. Before anyone knew quite what was happening, Anna had stopped and was gazing at a large watercolour of a sandy beach with spring flowers scattered amid wild grasses all around a deserted bay. "But you already have one of my paintings, so how can that possibly be? Now they were all staring at the painting. "That's just incredible," answered Corinne. "And even more so when I tell you it was a gift from Claude, our family solicitor, also a close friend of your father and a regular visitor to Scilly. He

must have visited your gallery and bought it from you! Michael admired it after the reading of Robin and Margo's wills, so Claude gave it to us and we presented it to Laura and Ben," she explained. I know this is going to sound completely bizarre, but it's as if your watercolours have been drawing you towards your father in some inexplicable way," continued Corinne.
"It was your painting of Cromwell's Castle that was spotted by George Simpkins and eventually led him and his colleague right to your door," she pointed out. Laura agreed there was more going on than they would ever know. "And dear old Albany House has certainly had more than its fair share of unbelievable coincidences, since the arrival of the Jameson family," she reminded everyone. A moments silence fell over the family gathering. "I think this might be the appropriate moment to say that as my father and my aunt Margo had such a profound influence on all of your lives, I have no desire to benefit from his legacy to me and would be very happy for it to be transferred to his charitable fund," she announced. But Luke's thoughts were already on tomorrow and of picking up Anna's student daughter Josie from Tiverton Parkway. He'd always been particularly close to Uncle Robin and the thought of meeting his step granddaughter was making him feel

quite emotional. It was dear Uncle Robin, who had first inspired him to help fight climate change when, as kids, he and Lottie had watched a news item about forest fires burning out of control in Australia. It was also earlier on that unforgettable afternoon, they'd been invited around for tea and, right out of the blue, that he and Auntie Margo had presented mum and dad with the keys to Albany House, because the young Jameson family had brought so much joy into their lives.

The Exeter train pulled in right on time and, to his surprise, only one young woman carrying a heavy bag emerged from the end carriage and began walking slowly along the platform towards him.

She was slim with short dark hair and was looking hesitantly at him. As their eyes locked, she smiled and in that instant they both knew instinctively that something special was about to happened. Taking her bag, they began strolling towards the car and chatting about what she was studying at Exeter.

"I know this might sound like a bit of a random question, but what do you think about climate change?" he asked.

THE END

Printed in Great Britain
by Amazon